THE WITCH OF RAVENSWOOD

Gothic Classics

THE
WITCH OF RAVENSWORTH

by

George Brewer

Edited with a new introduction by
Allen Grove

CHICAGO:
VALANCOURT BOOKS

The Witch of Ravensworth by George Brewer
Originally published 1808
First Valancourt Books edition, June 2006

Library of Congress Cataloging-in-Publication Data

Brewer, George, b. 1766.
  The witch of Ravensworth / by George Brewer ; edited with a new
introduction by Allen Grove. -- 1st Valancourt Books ed.
      p. cm. -- (Gothic classics)
  Includes bibliographical references.
  ISBN 0-9766048-8-4
  I. Grove, Allen W. II. Title. III. Series.
  PR4161.B589W58 2006
  823'.6--dc22
                                        2006012214

Published by Valancourt Books
Chicago, Illinois
www.valancourtbooks.com

Cover design by Ryan Cagle

Printed in the United States of America

CONTENTS

INTRODUCTION

NEARLY two centuries after George Brewer's witch first terrorized British readers, she has finally returned to haunt us once again. *The Witch of Ravensworth* represents one of the earliest English novels to focus on the familiar witch of fairy tale—the shriveled woman with her single tooth, crooked nose, and stooped back. Published in 1808, the novel appeared at a time when the British presses were flooded with tales of terror. Scores of writers were churning out stories of dark castles and corrupt ecclesiastics as they attempted to cash in on the popularity of Gothic fiction and the successes of Ann Radcliffe and Matthew Lewis. Brewer's *Witch,* however, stands out from the majority of these paltry imitations. The novel takes the clichés of the genre and twists them in new and often unpredictable ways. Very little in the work turns out to be what the reader initially expects. Also, Brewer's innovative style—with its short, quick-paced sentences—marks a clear break from the lush, if not overwrought, prose of Radcliffe and so many of her imitators.

At the same time, fans of Radcliffe, Lewis, and other terror writers will find that *The Witch of Ravensworth* has all the essential trappings of the Gothic. Drawing from Horace Walpole's *The Castle of Otranto* and Shakespeare's *Macbeth,* Brewer begins with a supernatural prophecy that sets events in motion. The ensuing narrative includes all the elements of the genre that delighted readers in the Romantic period and still delight them today: midnight cabals, curses, a tyrannical patriarch, helpless heroines, long-buried secrets, mysterious orphans, rusted locks, elaborate disguises, communion with demons, and the ubiquitous "secret and subterraneous passage beneath the foundations of the castle."

The literary influences on Brewer's tale are many. For his Hag, Brewer could be drawing from the witches of fairy-tale, childhood stories, or plays such as Shakespeare's *Macbeth* and Thomas Middleton's *The Witch.* The Baron, who believes the spirits of darkness "could bestow on their favourites the gifts of wealth and of ambition," mirrors Christopher Marlowe's Faustus, Matthew Lewis' Ambrosio, and other over-reachers. The monk Velaschi, whose actions were "frequently enwrapped in a dark veil of mystery," immediately evokes the spectre of Radcliffe's Schedoni from *The Italian,* although Brewer will ultimately steer away from the anti-Catholicism that defined so much early Gothic literature. The medievalism of *The Witch*—with its jousting, tournaments, castles, and knights—was made fashionable by Thomas Leland's *Longsword, Earl of Salisbury* (1762) and Walpole's *The Castle of Otranto* (1764), and was still popular in Brewer's day, as we see by the success of Sir Walter Scott's poetry and Waverley novels.

Despite the many interesting features of *The Witch of Ravensworth,* both the novel and its author are nearly unknown today, even amongst scholars of Gothic fiction and the Romantic period. George Brewer was baptized in Westminster in 1766, and he spent his youth as a midshipman traveling the world. By 1791 he was a lieutenant in the Swedish navy. During the 1790s he abandoned his life at sea to study law and become an attorney. Why a London attorney would turn to Gothic novel writing is a question largely without an answer, but Brewer's publication history paints the portrait of a man with playful wit, wide-ranging literary tastes, and a love for writing in a variety of genres. Brewer published at least three plays, several political tracts, numerous oriental tales, a book on gallantry, a collection of stories for children illustrating Le Brun's *Passions,* and dozens of essays—some serious, some satirical—dealing with issues as wide-ranging as "On the Dread of Mad Dogs," "Chapter on the Use of Fools," and "Forgiveness and Revenge."

Brewer wrote at least two novels other than *The Witch of Ravensworth.* His first, *The History of Tom Weston* (1791), was modeled after Henry Fielding's *Tom Jones,* and the Preface to his second novel, *The Motto, or, The History of Bill Woodcock* (1795), cites "with veneration, the names of Fielding and Smollett." Brewer uses this same Preface to define what he sees as the purpose of a novel: "To give a faithful picture of real life, to convey instruction, to amuse, to involve the reader in adventure and vicissitude, to excite joy and grief, to cause the tear of sensibility to flow, and to awaken the mind to humanity and benevolence; and lastly, to give virtue its reward, is the business of a Novel." This type of sentimental framework certainly found an avid audience in the mideighteenth century, but Brewer's efforts may have come a generation too late. Neither of his books met with much success.

The Witch of Ravensworth strays widely from the "faithful picture of real life" Brewer attempted in his earlier novels. Perhaps Brewer turned away from the sentimentality of works like *Tom Jones, Joseph Andrews,* and *Peregrine Pickle* because he realized that the Gothic dominated the literary landscape at the turn of the century. It's also possible that Brewer simply had an affinity for the genre: he had already proven himself a fan of the Gothic's close relative, the Oriental tale. In 1796, early in his writing career, he published *Siamese Tales*, nine stories purportedly translated from the Siamese, and E. W. Pitcher suspects that Brewer may also be the author of the 1794 *Tales of Elam* and "The Tales of the Twelve Soobahs of Indostan," a long narrative that ran in the *European Magazine* from 1805-6.

Brewer's novel shares much with the mass-consumed and often reprobate entertainments that saturated the presses of the early nineteenth century. Some of its content aligns *The Witch of Ravensworth* with works modern scholars have labeled "male Gothic," particularly the novel's presentations of demonic worship, human sacrifice, and the undisguised sexual actions of the Baron and Alwena. At the same time, however, the novel's conclusion and its engagement with sentimental ideals link it more to the "female Gothic." The physiognomy of Lady Bertha presents her unquestionable sensibility: "her face was expressive of the purest chastity and dignity of mind, her eyes beamed with the glances of charity and mildness" and the "sweetness of her voice" leaves all who hear it in thoughtful silence. Where Matthew Lewis uses Antonia to mock and critique this type of immaculate woman of feeling, Brewer seems to endorse the idealized heroine, and he contrasts her to the haughty Baron who was "cruel, delighting in the combats of animals, insensible to pity, and regardless of the complaints and sufferings of the poor."

At first glance, the novel's representation of male and female roles appears disappointingly conventional. The Baron has all the freedoms of a patriarch, while the Lady Bertha is "never at ease but when employed in her domestic duties; and was never seen to smile, but when it was with satisfaction at having pleased her lord." Brewer contrasts Bertha with Alwena who "had forsaken the reserve and delicacy proper to her sex." But Brewer is never content with mere convention, and by the time we reach the novel's sensational conclusion, we find no such predictable portrait of female virtue. Alwena is indeed punished for her transgressions, but Brewer's "proper" women prove themselves to be capable of much more than domestic servitude. In fact, Brewer ultimately suggests that the wife, not the patriarch, governs the unfolding events.

Brewer's novel likewise has a level of moral instruction and social criticism that we do not find in Lewis' *The Monk*. For example, the novel comments on the disparity between the wealthy

Baron and Gerrard's poor, laboring cottage family. Brewer's interest in the unequal distribution of wealth and resulting abuse of power finds voice in two of his significant works on the topic: *The Rights of the Poor* (1800) and *Prospectus of A New Law between Debtor and Creditor* (1806). Thus, Brewer has not entirely abandoned the ideals of his earlier sentimental novels, for he uses the Gothic, at least in theory, to "awaken the mind to humanity and benevolence." As the haughty Baron learns that the fulfillment of his desires fails to bring him happiness, the reader learns the same lesson.

In fact, despite the Baron's constant cruelty, Brewer's novel paints an optimistic view of human nature. Through the Baron's child Hugo, the work suggest that ill behavior is the result of faulty nurture: "Hugo grew up with all the fierce dispositions of his father, who caressed him chiefly on that account: he was bold, mischievous, ill-tempered, and obstinate." Yet if an innocent child can be molded into a tyrant, Brewer also suggests the opposite: even a tyrant can be reformed and redeemed.

Brewer is not, however, a heavy-handed moralist, and some of his less serious essays find voice in *The Witch of Ravensworth*. Brewer, like many of his predecessors, presents his servant characters as the clowns and fools who provide comic relief from the heavy drama. Thus we get Doric the steward who constantly confuses himself with the study of mathematics, and Jonas the butler who lives in a constant state of inebriation, yet "had the art of being perfectly sober when he was drunk." The same year Brewer published *The Witch of Ravensworth,* he had explored this art in "The Art of Getting Drunk," where he notes that the people of Great Britain "have brought the art of drinking to perfection" by abiding to the rule that "a gentleman should always be sober when he is drunk." His praise of this talent concludes with the observation that the drunkard will find his behavior an "agreeable and pleasant . . . system of suicide."

Deborah, another of Brewer's lower-class characters, has a vice of her own: her "longing for riches, which . . . appeared to her the greatest blessing in life." We learn that Deborah would "like dearly to be rich, and to have a castle, and forests, and deer, . . . and plenty of servants." She even claims she would "never scold [her] poor Gerrard again" if she had wealth. Her attitude resonates with Brewer's humorous essay, "The Pocket Remedy," in which he satirically presents a guinea as the universal panacea for any ailment or social ill.

Deborah will get her wish when her husband Gerrard unexpectedly finds himself heir to a fortune. The resulting scene is one of the more original and provocative in the novel, for Brewer avoids the typical rags-to-riches wish-fulfillment so common in the Gothic. One need only think of Theodore in *Otranto,* Edmund in *The Old English Baron,* Ellena in *The Italian* to recognize the prominence of the reversal-of-fortune plot. In all of these texts, however, the poor cottagers turn out to be displaced nobility. Gerrard is what he seems to be—a simple, unpolished wood-cutter. This makes his speech to the tenantry all the more remarkable:

> Friends and neighbours, Providence has so ordered it, that a poor wood-cutter should become your lord. There be many who would find it difficult to do their duty in a station so much above them: I shall not; I shall be just and honest, and it must go hard indeed, if things turn out amiss. You shall all be rich in the best comforts of life, and the poor man shall never want bread . . . I shall give judgment among you fairly. I have not much learning, 'tis true, yet, I know that there is but the right and the wrong, and that it is not so easy to mistake one for the other, as many people would try to make us believe.

This speech would have a very different meaning in the early 1790s than in 1808. What Brewer presents with Gerrard and Deborah is a new social order in which law, order, and a fair distribution of wealth are made a reality through governance by the working classes. The ideals here are very much the same ones that drove the storming of the Bastille in 1789 and fueled the early days of the French Revolution.

By 1808, however, writers who had first romanticized and idealized the Revolution had witnessed it turn into a bloodbath with tyranny and horrors far surpassing those that had come before. Indeed, by 1808 the English had watched Napoleon rise to power and push an entire continent into war. The resulting violence frequently found voice in Gothic novels, such as when Matthew Lewis in *The Monk* pens a gruesome scene of the common masses rioting and murdering innocent nuns. Brewer, however, moves in the opposite direction and suggests, long after the failures of the Revolution were clear, that the impoverished masses could, in fact, govern justly. In the final pages Brewer will back away from this position and restores governance to the nobility, but Gerrard's speech still appears remarkable within its historical context.

The conclusion of *The Witch of Ravensworth* is, to say the least, bizarre. Much in the novel remains unresolved, and as with many Gothic fictions of the day, we are forced to overlook obvious inconsistencies between the bulk of the narrative and the eventual resolution. Does the final outcome justify the elaborate scheming and even cruelty of the Lady Gertrude? Is the Baron really a redeemable character? Are we really supposed to view Alwena's fate as insignificant? Frederick Frank notes that "the Baron's crimes and murders accumulate until Brewer, realizing that he had too many unburied bodies scattered about his contorted plot, resorts to incredible coincidence to wrench the story back into line" (35). Such narrative contrivances were a hallmark of the Gothic long before Brewer's work, having been so conventional that Jane Austen mocked them in the late 1790s in *Northanger Abbey:* "my readers, who will see in the tell-tale compression of the pages before them, that we are all hastening together to perfect felicity." And indeed, Austen quickly explains away all the novel's mysteries and makes a Viscount magically appear to marry one of her heroines.

Whatever the contrivances of Brewer's conclusion, however, it does not have the feeling of either Austen or the source of her parody, Ann Radcliffe's *The Mysteries of Udolpho*. Where Ann Radcliffe, Clara Reeve, and Regina Maria Roche tend to conclude with happily-ever-after portraits of home and hearth, Brewer provides no such closure. Nor does he leave us with the melancholic contentment that defines the ending of Walpole's *The Castle of Otranto*, or the violent damnation of Matthew Lewis' Ambrosio. What we do get is a reversal of the novel's power structure as the central women topple the haughty Baron. Brewer ultimately makes his reader reevaluate labels such as "mad," "hag," and "witch," and recognize that such terms may simply describe rebellious, nonconforming, strong women who refuse to be destroyed by patriarchal abuses.

The Valancourt Books edition of *The Witch of Ravensworth* is based on the 1808 two-volume first edition of the novel, published by J. F. Hughes of London. I have preserved the idiosyncrasies of the original: missing and extraneous apostrophes, inconsistent spellings ("stampt" and "stamped"), haphazard comma usage, and Brewer's apparent fondness for run-on sentences. I added a few quotation marks where necessary for clarity, and at the end of the first volume I substituted the word "termination" for "determination," the latter being an obvious error in the original printing. Aside from these few minor corrections, the text of this new Valancourt edition is identical to that which readers enjoyed two centuries ago. Gothic fiction has transformed significantly during those two hundred years, and Brewer's Hag deserves her rightful place in that literary history. While Brewer's contemporaries continued to recycle stories of corrupt monks and abusive tyrants, *The Witch of Ravensworth* marks a shift to the Gothic masterpieces of the nineteenth century. His Hag has little in common with eighteenth-century villainesses such as Lewis' Matilda or Radcliffe's Marchesa. In fact, the witch's moral ambiguity and physical monstrosity link her more directly to the Gothic's most famous monster in Frankenstein, a creature Mary Shelley would not create for another decade.

ALLEN GROVE

Alfred, New York
April 8, 2006

ABOUT THE EDITOR

Allen Grove (Ph.D. University of Pennsylvania) is Associate Professor of English at Alfred University where he teaches courses such as Tales of Terror, Gothic Fiction, and The Romantic Movement. His research and teaching often explore the interplay between sexuality, science, and genre in Gothic fiction. He has authored several articles and reviews on eighteenth- and nineteenth-century literature. He is the editor of *The Cavern of Death* for Valancourt Books, a teaching edition of Ann Radcliffe's *The Italian* for College Publishing, and he is currently working on H. G. Wells's *The Invisible Man* for Broadview Press.

WORKS BY GEORGE BREWER

"The Art of Getting Drunk." *The European Magazine* (July 1808): 18-21.

Bannian Day, A Musical Entertainment, in Two Acts. London: T. N. Longman, 1796.

The History of Tom Weston, A Novel, After the Manner of Tom Jones. 2 vols. London: T. Hookham, 1791.

Hours of Leisure; or, Essays and Characteristics. London: J. Hatchard, 1806.

How to be Happy, A Comedy in Five Acts. 1794.

How to Be Happy, or, The Agreeable Hours of Human Life Being a Series of Essays on the Influences which Produce Happiness. London: W. M. Thiselton, 1814.

The Juvenile Lavater, or, A Familiar Explanation of the Passions of Le Brun: Calculated for the Instruction and Entertainment of Young Persons. London: Minerva Press, 1812.

The Life of Rolla: a Peruvian Tale: With Moral Inculcations for Youth: Including, A Description of the Temple of the Sun. The Mysteries of the Golden Leaf. The Seven Springs in the Valley of Nanasca. The Story of the Tree with One Branch. The Story of the Inca who Wept Blood. The Speech of Rolla. The Battle of Quito. The Death of Rolla. London: E. Newbery, 1800.

The Man in the Moon: A Dramatic Sketch in One Act. 1799.

Maxims of Gallantry, or the History of the Count de Verney. London: Hookham and Carpenter, 1793.

The Motto: or History of Bill Woodcock. 2 vols. London: G. Sael, 1795.

"The Pocket Remedy." *The European Magazine* (May 1807): 358-9.

Prospectus of a New Law Between Debtor and Creditor: With Remarks on the Inefficacy of Imprisonment for Debt, and its Injury to Commerce and Trade. London: W. Clarke, 1806.

The Rights of the Poor Considered; With the Causes and Effects of Monopoly, and a Plan of Remedy by Means of a Popular Progressive Excise. London: J. Debrett, 1800.

The Siamese Tales, Being a Collection of Stories Told to the Son of the Mandarin Sam-Sib, for the Purpose of Engaging his Mind in the Love of Truth and Virtue, with an Historical Account of the Kingdom of Siam, to which is added The Principle Maxims of the Talapoins. London: Vernor and Hood, 1796.

FURTHER READING

A Biographical Dictionary of the Living Authors of Great Britain and Ireland. London: Henry Colburn, 1816. 37-8.

Botting, Fred. *Gothic*. London: Routledge, 1996.

Clery, E. J. *The Rise of Supernatural Fiction, 1762-1800.* Cambridge: Cambridge University Press, 1995.

Ellis, Kate Ferguson. *The Contested Castle: Gothic Novels and the Subversion of Domestic Ideology*. Urbana: University of Illinois Press, 1989.

Frank, Frederick S. *The First Gothics: A Critical Guide to the English Gothic Novel*. New York: Garland, 1987.

Hoeveler, Diane Long. *Gothic Feminism: The Professionalization of Gender from Charlotte Smith to the Brontës*. University Park, Pa.: University of Pennsylvania Press, 1998.

Humphreys, Jennet. "George Brewer." Oxford Dictionary of National Biography. Oxford: Oxford University Press, 2004-6. 1 Jan. 2006. <http://www.oxforddnb.com>.

Miles, Robert. *Gothic Writing 1750-1820: A Genealogy*. London: Routledge, 1993.

Pitcher, E. W. "On Authorship of Essay Serials in the *European Magazine* and *The Lady's Monthly Museum:* George Brewer and G. Bedingfield." Notes and Queries 44.2 (June 1997): 238-239.

---. "The Miscellaneous Publications of George Brewer (1766-1816?)" *The Library* 4 (1982): 320-323.

Sedgwick, Eve Kosofsky. *The Coherence of Gothic Conventions*. New York: Methuen, 1986.

Summers, Montague. *The Gothic Quest: A History of the Gothic Novel*. 1938. New York: Russell & Russell, 1966.

Varma, Devendra P. *The Gothic Flame*. New York: Russell & Russell, 1966.

Watson, Melvin R. *Magazine Serials and the Essay Tradition 1746-1820*. Baton Rouge: Louisiana State University Press, 1956.

Williams, Ann. *Art of Darkness: A Poetics of Gothic*. Chicago: University of Chicago Press, 1995.

THE

WITCH

OF

RAVENSWORTH;

A ROMANCE,

IN TWO VOLUMES.

By *GEORGE BREWER*,
AUTHOR OF " HOURS OF LEISURE."

VOL. I.

LONDON:
PRINTED FOR J. F. HUGHES, 15, PATER-NOSTER-ROW,
AND 5, WIGMORE-STREET, CAVENDISH-SQUARE.

1808.

CHAPTER I

Description of the Hag.

ON the extremity of a wild heath, known by the name of Ravens-worth-Moor, in the county of Westmoreland; and in or about the time of the second crusade, stood a miserable hut, consisting but of one open to the rafters; which were in fact nothing more than rough-hewn poles sloping from the wall, covered with soot, and curiously embossed with cobwebs. The chimney was little else than a large hole made in the side, for the smoke to issue; and the window, if it could be called one, was so completely stuffed with hay, to keep out the weather, that but a few particles of light could be seen through the aperture.

Yet in this miserable hovel lived one solitary human being, an old woman named Ann Ramsay, but better known by the title of the Hag. She was little, thin, bent almost double, and very aged; her flesh was of a dark brown, and so lean and skinny, that it hung in a variety of folds from her arms; her face was wrinkled all over; her eyes small, and the sockets red, as if inflamed by disease, or anger; her head was long, and sunk between her shoulders; her nose was prominent and crooked, besides that it was constantly smeared with snuff; her lips were pale, and her single tooth, for she appeared to have but one, stood projecting its black arc over the front of her wide mouth: in short, she was so horribly ugly, that no one would come within two yards of her, when she approached. Such was the faithful portrait of the Hag of Ravensworth.

The furniture of the cottage of dame Ramsay, was well suited to her miserable dwelling: it consisted of a straw mattress rolled up in one corner of the room, and covered over with a dirty and ragged rug, an antient carved wainscot-table, and a three-legged stool, always placed by the fire-side, and on which the old witch used to sit; a broken piece of glass, of a diagonal form, with a small remnant of quicksilver, placed upon the basso relievo of a part of the wall, its plaster mouldering with age; a pitcher, a birch-broom, and a large iron kettle, or cauldron, completed the inventory of the effects in this wretched hovel.

The Hag might be seen, sitting on her three-legged stool, the greater part of the day, bent nearly double, with her elbows fixed upon her knees, and her chin resting upon the props made for it by the palms of her hands. It was in this attitude that it was supposed

3

Dame Ramsay designed her mischievous machinations, as it was then that frequent unintelligible utterings were heard to come from her lips, by such as happened to pass near: at these times, the witch appeared to be either threatening or blaspheming. Indeed there were not any who entertained the smallest doubt, of such appearances being caused by her being engaged in communications with the evil spirit.

In the opposite corner, by the fire-side, was usually seen seated, and looking the Hag full in the face, a large, meagre, slender grey cat, the constant companion of her evenings. The body of this creature was of an uncommon length, its neck and loins pinched in with want, its eyes large and full, starting, as it were, from the sockets, its immense whiskers were constantly spread abroad, as to scent the blood which it was its delight to lap, its tall slender legs raised it above the usual size of those animals, and its long talons could draw, with ease, the flesh from the tortured rat which had become its prey.

A large black raven was also an inhabitant of this miserable dwelling, and might be seen hopping about the floor, and flapping one of its large jetty wings, the other being cut close to prevent its excursions on the heath.

The Hag Ramsay was so much the terror of all the country round about, for several miles, that neither man, woman, nor child, would pass near that part of the moor, on the borders of which was her dwelling, unless it were from absolute necessity, or from an ignorance of the road. It was current among the poor people of the nearest village, that the witch of Ravensworth had come invisibly to take possession of the hut, which had been empty for a great many years; the tradition was, that nobody knew how she had come thither, nor from whence she came; that she appeared all at once; that she had no father nor mother; that she had no relations; that she had given herself the name of Ann Ramsay, but that she had never been known to be called by any other appellation, than that of the Hag.

Many were the strange stories related by the country people, of this extraordinary woman, and out of number, the instances of her powers of witchcraft. It was stated by them, that innumerable children had been missed by their parents, in the neighbourhood of the Hag, and had never been seen or heard of afterwards. They were ready to swear to their belief of these infants having been carried away by the witch Ramsay, and destroyed. It was, besides, currently reported, and attested by many, that the Hag's inclination was to feed on the flesh of young babes; and the cries of little children, being whipped or tortured to death by her, had been frequently heard.

It was in vain that the wardens of the forest had endeavoured to bring the witch of Ravensworth to justice: there was not any thing, that could be established by certain testimony against her, although the presumptive proofs were strong enough to convince all. It was necessary, however, that witnesses should support the circumstantial evidence, from their own knowledge of facts; such evidence was not, however, easily obtained. One man, who had ventured to bring a charge of witchcraft against her, was stated to have been seized with dreadful convulsions in the audience-chamber, at the very instant he was about to open his mouth, and soon after expired, without being able to give his testimony. Another, who had spoken of her wicked arts, became suddenly possest of an evil spirit; and a third was reported to have been struck dumb by her potency in the black art. Her skill in magic was, indeed, stated to be such, that she could with ease transform and alter the features of man, woman, or child, in so great a degree, that they could not be known even by their nearest relations, and that she could, if she pleased, change any, who were weak enough to offend her, into loathsome reptiles, such as bats, or efts, or lizards; in short, every one felt horror and terror, at the bare mention of the name of the hag, and the blood of the boldest villagers turned chill at her approach. Many never recovered, who had met her in the lane by accident, and some, who had been rash enough to visit her hut, had never been known to return.

Even the air, surrounding the dwelling of the hag, was pestiferous: snakes, vipers, and large loathsome worms, might be observed gliding through the rank weeds, and about the dunghill at her door; and, in summer days, a toad of the largest size might be seen basking itself in the full sunshine at the threshold of her hovel.

The herds of cattle and sheep, which fed nigh the dwelling of the witch, were said to die daily of the rot; and round the hut itself, not even a blade of grass would grow. The other cottages on the heath had little gardens attached to them, in which might be seen the rose and the jessamine, with the wholesome vegetable for the humble board of their owners; but the hovel of the Hag was a waste piece of ground, filled with hemlock, and other poisonous, rank, and unwholesome weeds; a stagnant pool was in the midst, over which myriads of the transparent-winged Libellulæ might be seen darting from side to side. The dearth around this spot was no other way accounted for, than that it was near the dwelling of a witch; while, though the other cottages belonged to poor people, yet they were honest.

CHAPTER II

An account of the Baron de La Braunch.

WITHIN the distance of a mile westward of the hut of the Hag, amidst an assemblage of hills, and falls, shadowed on the side by an extensive forest, stood the castle of *La Braunch*, accessible only by its draw-bridges, of which there were seven in number.

The scenery around was grand and majestic. The thick-bodied oak, and the tall fir, stood stately above the other trees, a fall from the rapid and impetuous river Eden, enriched the landscape, and the numerous flocks of sheep, which covered the surrounding fields, presented, at once, a picture of the wealth and happiness of the soil.

The castle of La Braunch, had been built by one of the ancestors of the baron, about the time of the Norman conquest, and was the only part left, of the patrimony which he had received from his father.

The Baron de La Braunch was remarkable for the height of his stature, which measured more than seven feet six inches, his limbs were formed with a fine, though athletic, proportion, his eyes were large and full, and beamed with the strong glances of pride and defiance; his countenance was ferocious, and the smile which sometimes appeared, was little else than the sarcastic expression of contempt, or of scorn; when he walked, he trod on the ground with a firmness, and dignity, that commanded awe and respect.

The Baron de La Braunch bore his head with a lofty superiority, above the other knights and barons of the court of Edward.

The baron was the heir of a parent who had squandered away nearly the whole of his fortune, in the lavish and profuse expenses of his household and table, and at play. The greater part of his princely fortune, had been lost at the game of chess, a favourite amusement of the knights of the *crusade,* when relieved from the duties of the soldier.

The baron was educated under the care of the monk Velaschi.

The monk Velaschi was a perfect judge of the human heart, and knew all its folds and recesses, he was master of an uncommon share of prudence, and of reserve; none could decide upon his actions, which at times appeared noble and disinterested, but more frequently were enwrapped in a dark veil of mystery, that seemed to conceal some malignant design, or mischief. Velaschi was a scholar, and skilled in the cabalistic art. There were very few, but who, while they courted his friendship, trembled for fear of his displeasure. They knew the high favour in which he stood with the greatest barons of the time, and the means he had to do them service, or Velaschi would have been neglected, or shunned, as the object of mistrust and dread.

Such was the monk Velaschi, and such the master of the baron, who, as he grew to manhood, became the slave of an inordinate ambition; he had, however, at an early age found the way to bend his haughty and determined spirit to his views, whether from the ingenious precepts of the monk, or from his natural character, could not be easily developed; he had accustomed himself to smile alike at the contempt, the esteem, or the hatred, of the world; any means appeared to the Baron de La Braunch as praiseworthy, which could lead to the circumstances of fortune: cowardly, yet rash; vindictive, overbearing, and ambitious, yet, when it suited his purpose, kind and courteous; haughty to those from whom he expected nothing, and abject and mean enough to submit to any thing, from those whose protection and favour he wished to obtain. Not yet bold enough, of himself, to commit great crimes, but depraved enough at all times to be willing to commit them, whenever the fear of detection did not prevent him. Base, grand, mean, and proud; the baron showed those strong impulses and dispositions of mind, which, well directed, might make him famed, or infamous. In a word the Baron de La Braunch was a complete and high-finished Hypocrite, and to such a degree of perfection, through the diabolical maxims he had established, had he brought the art of dissimulation, that he could affect mildness, sensibility, or forgiveness, at the very instant that his mind was raging with the most discordant passions, enmities, and enormities of thought of which the human heart is incapable.

The Baron de La Braunch was a master in the art of deception, and a coward at heart; he had, nevertheless, owed many of the honours he had received, to the display of an undaunted prowess;

for though mean enough to take every unfair, or cruel advantage, yet he was, when compelled to fight, desperate in encounter, and had signalized himself much at the holy war; his figure was indeed of the noblest stature, his strength prodigious. The buckler which he bore, made of osier, was of uncommon dimensions, and on its surface was carved and painted a lion, enraged, and springing on his prey. His casque, which was of gold, bore a crest of horse-hair dyed red, and the arms he carried were the javelin, and a ponderous battle-ax. In the field, at the tournament, and in the crusade, the Baron de La Braunch was esteemed a brave and gallant knight. At home, and among his vassals, he was known to be mistrustful, suspicious, and cruel, delighting in the combats of animals, insensible to pity, and regardless of the complaints and sufferings of the poor.

The Baron de La Braunch had never married, though a confused tale of his infidelity to a lady of the name of Gertrude was sometimes spoken of, but there were not any who seemed to be sufficiently acquainted with facts, to relate how that matter had terminated.

The baron, whose proud and overbearing spirit could not brook the superior condition of other knights, suffered continually the most agonizing and severe reflections on the insufficiency of his fortune to support the high rank he held.

Thus, then, wealth was the great object of his ambition, and his lively and turbulent imagination was never at rest an instant, on a subject which he considered so material to his happiness; he therefore promised to himself the full possession of his darling wish, though to be purchased at any price.

At length the brightest star in the baron's horoscope, shone forth in its full radiance; he saw, and found means to ingratiate himself into the favour of, lady Bertha, the relict of the brave and rich lord Edward of Martindale, who was killed in the second crusade, after sustaining the combat with two infidel chiefs for more than two hours and a half, and after having slain one of them and wounded the other.

The lady Bertha was of a tall majestic figure, her form every thing that could be imagined of symmetry and grace, her face was expressive of the purest chastity and dignity of mind, her eyes beamed with the glances of charity and mildness, her manners were the most gentle and courteous, and when she spoke, the sweetness of her discourse was such, that every one dwelt in silence upon her utterance. The lady Bertha appeared more an angel than a woman, and her surpassing virtues, ranked her among the first of the ladies of the British court.

Lady Bertha had had one child, a male, by her late Lord, and which was born a few months before the death of its father. This infant was the tender object of her care, and it was in consequence of the situation of the child, that she sought the friendship of the Baron de La Braunch, who, under the colour of that sacred character, sought to improve the suit he had in view.

The baron however showed so much kind attention to the infant, and paid so high a respect to the lady Bertha, that she suffered his approaches without suspicion of the design he had formed the very first instant he had beheld her, and which lurked in his bosom, waiting only a fit opportunity for its execution.

The baron, versed in all the arts of falsehood, and skilled in persuasion, found means, at length, to make the lady Bertha believe, that the love he professed for her was honest and sincere, that it was grounded on friendship and esteem, and, as the strongest inducement, urged that the best protection she could give her child, would be to confide it to the care of a man of his high character, and consequence at court.

The pride, and known prowess of the baron de La Braunch, kept at a distance the other numerous knights, who would gladly have made offers of their hands to lady Bertha; he watched her so closely, and attended so assiduously to her, that no opportunity was left for the less adventurous; the baron therefore courted the lady Bertha unmolested, and with success.

A month had scarcely elapsed beyond the usual and proper time for ladies to mourn for their deceased knights, before the baron obtained a promise of her hand, nor before a day was fixed for the actual celebration of the nuptials.

CHAPTER III

Preparations for a Wedding.

THE household of the Baron de La Braunch, consisted of the following characters. Hathbrand, his esquire; a servile and cringing courtier, devoted to the interests of his master, and warped from every sentiment of honesty and honour, by the promises and prospects held out to his ambition. The noble frankness required, and resulting properly from the nature of man, had yielded to a tacit and contemptible obedience.

Doric, the old steward, purveyor and superintendant of the castle; honest enough, but so from mere habit, and the necessity required by his condition for that virtue. The mind of Doric was, besides the daily performances of his duty, constantly engaged in the study of the mathematics, with which he confused himself at times to such a degree, that his disorder appeared very like drunkenness. Doric was for measuring every thing by the square and cube; and as the baron was much too lofty to look at any one of his household below his esquire, or to observe their actions, old Doric was left at liberty to study geometry and trigonometry, as much as he pleased.

The next servant of consequence, in the castle of La Braunch, was Jonas the butler, who, happily for him, had the art of being perfectly sober when he was drunk; that is, by habit, he always appeared cool and collected, let the degree of his inebriation be what it might. This presence of mind was necessary in the presence of the baron, of whom Doric, as well as the rest of the domestics, stood very much in fear. Jonas never looked so wise, nor talked so wise, as when he had taken liberal potions of wine.

The meaner dependants of the castle were numerous, and the entire vassals of their lord.

The female attendants were, old Ruth the housekeeper, Guinefred the waiting-woman, hired on purpose to attend the lady Bertha, and numerous other domestics and servants, whose duty it would be to serve their new mistress.

Guinefred was a virtuous and honest domestic, which qualities the baron never suspected she possessed, as she appeared so perfectly humble that he thought her a creature fitted for the station he designed her, from the awe and respect with which she viewed her master, and the implicit obedience she paid to his inclinations and commands.

The greatest preparations ever known at the castle of La Braunch, were now making for the reception of the lady Bertha. Hathbrand was engaged in procuring from all parts of the kingdom the richest jewels, and ornaments of apparel, for the bride of the baron his master: Doric, the old steward, did not neglect, on his part, to make the necessary searches and researches in the cellar, for the choicest wines; and the flaggons were already filled with rhenish and burgundy.

Old Ruth the housekeeper, had prepared the most delectable fruits and preserves, and Guinefred, on her part, was engaged night and day, in making ready for the display of the magnificent wardrobe, which the munificence of the baron had ordained for his consort.

Old Doric and Jonas were however the most rejoiced of the family, at the thought of the approaching event; they had, for so many years, witnessed only the gloomy grandeur of the castle, and the reserve and haughty demeanour of their master, that they were almost frantic at the change likely to take place so soon. The baron's manners, too, were altered to his domestics, he smiled graciously when he gave his commands, and mentioned the name of his intended bride, with such affection and respect, that they anticipated a house, and season of joy. What made them most sure of this, was, that the baron had given orders that the castle should be open for a month to every stranger, and that his tenantry and vassals should be entertained during that period. Few or none of these had experienced any munificence before, and the conjecture was, that the baron was, in truth, a good and liberal master, but that his wealth had been insufficient to the noble bent of his nature.

The castle itself assumed a different appearance. The seven draw-bridges had been raised, and every gate was thrown open to the traveller, the pilgrim, and the minstrel. The bugles were sounded night and morning from the battlements, and the approach of the gay and happy time that was to celebrate the nuptials of the baron de La Braunch was announced by the music of the clarion, the virginal, and the trumpet.

CHAPTER IV

The Bridal Day.

EARLY in the morning of the bridal day, the servants and vassals of the baron were industriously employed in preparing the Gothic hall of the castle for the reception of their lady. The trophies and banners, the achievements of the baron, were displayed from the arched roof, and the swords, battle-axes, and lances, crossed in various devices against the wall. The tables were spread with the most sumptuous and noble fare, and the most delicious wines were ready to be served. Every domestic was dressed for the occasion: old Doric had studied a proper mathematical arrangement, in the disposition of the tables, chairs, and lights, and Jonas seemed to have made a reserve of intellect, sufficient to enjoy the gradations of the coming festivity.

The morning was fine, and the landscape gay with the fresh verdure of the spring: Nature seemed pleased with the joy that was revived among the honest villagers surrounding the castle, and as unwilling to disturb, by lowering clouds, or inclemency, their promised sports.

About the hour of twelve at noon, when the shining beams of the sun gilded with their full radiance the turrets of the castle of La Braunch, the bride and her train of attendants were announced, by the distant sound of the bugle in the still air, which was answered from the battlements, and at a distance, winding round the hills, were seen the cavalcade bearing the banners of the lady's former lord. The baron de La Braunch, preceded by minstrels, and attended by twenty knights, went out to meet the bride. Among the number of these were, Bertrand the bold, of gigantic stature, who bore the device of the blazing star on his shield, and whose helmet was of gold. Alerias a renowned knight of Gaul, of small stature, but so active, that by his agility and prowess he had discomfited six knights at tournaments. Palmerin the accomplished, who spoke seven languages, managed the horse with consummate skill, and threw the lance from his hand with such dexterity that it was seldom known to miss. Athelbert the strong, who could wield an iron bar of many cubits, with as much ease as a common spear. Roderic the brave, of the red cross. Roland the noble; and indeed all of them were knights famed in chivalry, and of great prowess.

The bride approached, attended by twelve ladies, and followed by twelve knights and their esquires, bearing in the midst of them, above their own devices, the banner which displayed the device of the fierce and terrible dragon destroyed by the hand of the father of the lady Bertha, who was a brave knight, and who had defeated several champions of England and France at different tournaments.

The Infant child, the son of lady Bertha by her late lord, lord Edward of Martindale, was borne on a litter on which was a bed of the finest linen, covered with a canopy of rich silk, wrought with gold; three attendants on each side, threw flowers, and sprinkled rich perfumes over the infant as it lay, at the same time the minstrels sung the melodies of joy; the servants and vassals of the late lord Edward followed the train.

The trumpets and bugles sounded, when the two parties met, and the baron advancing his white courser to the palfrey of lady Bertha, took his helmet from his head, and, extending his arm, saluted his bride with the grace peculiar to a courteous knight. The lady Bertha at the same time touching her fingers with her lips, and extending her hand, received the baron; when at the side of his bride he turned his horse toward the castle, and his train joined that of his lady.

The domestics of the castle, who knew of the approach of the party, by the sound of the trumpets, as they passed the draw-bridges, ranged themselves on each side the gothic hall, and the numerous tenantry without, rent the air with their rejoicings.

The ceremony of the marriage took place in the chapel belonging to the castle, and was performed by father Velaschi, who could not help viewing the bride with admiration and esteem.

CHAPTER V

The Wedding Dinner.—The uninvited Guest.

THE sounds of the cymbal, the clarion, and the trumpet, announced that the baron and the lady Bertha were just seated at the table.

The lady Bertha was on the right of the baron, clothed in white silk, her fine auburn hair bound with a fillet of gold-work; on her right shoulder was placed the escutcheon of the baron, and on the left that of her own family.

The baron de La Braunch was in complete armour; he had a belt round him, on which were devices of frightful and terrible animals; his cloak, which was thrown over his shoulders, was blue and gold, and a plume of red feathers was in his helmet, which was placed beside him; he bore on his buckler the motto of his father, who had often conquered at Palestine. It was EO TRIOMPHE.

The lady of each knight was seated next her husband, sumptuously arrayed; nor was there any thing that could exceed the grandeur and brilliancy of this banquet. The golden vases, which decorated the board, were each of them filled with the richest Burgundy and Rhenish, and every cup was also of gold. The meats were of the most savoury and exquisite kinds, and the greatest care had been taken to provide for the noble guests every thing that was rare, and the produce of foreign climes.

Delight and joy were upon every countenance, and the minstrels played and sung their most popular ballads together, with some written in honour of the illustrious bride, and which were received with rapturous applause.

The windows and doors had been thrown open, to let in the soft breezes of the summer south wind; and in the outer halls, were the vassals of the baron, regaling themselves with unusual festivity.

A delightful day added to the pleasure of the scene. The guests at the baron's table were all in harmony with each other, and nothing was heard, but the gentle dialogue of courtesy and invitation.

One seat only had remained unoccupied at the board, and one plate only was covered. Some knight had neglected the invitation, but that was a circumstance scarcely noticed by any present, and which did not at all interfere with the festivity of the guests.

At a moment when the conversation had had a pause, and when every ear was engaged in listening to the sweet plaintive measures of a ballad sung by a minstrel, the harmony of the meeting was interrupted.

A loud shriek was heard from the lower end of the table.

Terror was in every face.

The music stopped.

The singer ceased his melody.

All was surprise and terror.

The vacant chair was filled.

It was a wretched misshapen figure that occupied the seat.

It was wrapped up in a black mantle and hood, which covered all but a pale meagre face, so ugly that no eye could look upon it.

It had taken a golden cup from the board, and had raised it to its lips.

It drank—not a health—not a blessing.—It uttered a curse—a horrid curse:—"Misery to the Bride."

All eyes were turned at once, but for an instant only on the loathsome object.

It kept its seat.

It smiled.

It was recognised.

It was the Hag.

The lady Bertha, as soon as the imprecation came from the lips of the witch, fainted away in the arms of her attendants; while the baron, in a stern voice, that made tremble the foundation of the castle, demanded how the Hag had found an entrance to her presence, and, in a lofty tone, ordered her instantly to depart.

The Hag arose, and walked slowly from the table.

In going out, the witch turned round, and looked sternly at the baron.

The Hag burst into a loud convulsive laugh.

She muttered some imprecations to herself.

She withdrew.

The Hag had no sooner left the hall than the beautiful face of day became overcast, large black clouds arose swiftly from the horizon, and the big drops of rain beat in torrents against the gothic casements.

The festivity of the guests was at an end,—a pause of doubt, and of astonishment, continued for a considerable time.—It was in vain that father Velaschi used his pious ejaculations to overcome the impression the malediction of the witch had made on the guests.

The lady Bertha had withdrawn with her attendants, after receiving every consolation and encouragement the courteous manners of the company could suggest.

The baron, immediately after his bride withdrew with the other ladies, scoffing at the interruption which had occurred, poured out copious draughts of Burgundy, to enliven himself and his guests, which answered better to restore festivity than all father Velaschi's pious exhortations.

The recollection of the Hag was drowned in plentiful libations, and loud and riotous mirth succeeded, in which was lost every other sensation; and the ill-timed visit of the uninvited and unexpected guest, troubled them no more.

CHAPTER VI

The baron recollects the circumstances of the Hag's intrusion and reflects.

THE next day, the baron withdrew to his closet, that he might recollect the circumstances of the Hag's intrusion. There he gave a serious consideration to the mystery of her visit, and to the nature of her imprecation. At first, indeed, in the natural fierceness of his temper, and impetuosity, he would have dispatched the wardens of the forest to have seized the old wretch, and to have brought her to immediate justice; he paused, however, and on reflection found reason to alter his mind. The intrusion of the Hag was an heinous offence, but the curse that had come from her lips was not for him; he knew, indeed, that he ought, out of courtesy to lady Bertha, to make a parade of punishing the witch, but he had no desire to let it go further than mere threat: orders for her apprehension were therefore issued, and countermanded with the same breath.

The baron, however, soothed the distressed mind of lady Bertha with every kind and endearing expression of love and affection, and assured her of his desire to punish and remove every object that could give her uneasiness; somehow, notwithstanding this apparent promptness to punish the offender, he certainly entertained a secret desire to know more of her. Whether he contemplated the possibility of the Hag being one day or other useful to him, or whether, being naturally superstitious, he wished to be acquainted with the mystery of her visit, or with the secrets of her art, it was not easy to judge; something however certainly constrained him from awarding to her the immediate punishment which his natural proud and impatient temper would have suggested in any other case.

The baron used more than common assiduities to overcome the impression made on the mind of his lady, by the mysterious visit of the witch; he indeed attempted to persuade her, that that wicked old woman was mad, and that she did not know what she had said; he took also a great deal of pains to premise to his attendants and domestics the fact of her insanity, and then artfully inquired of them, their opinion as to the real or pretended madness of the Hag, and which he was sure would, thus prepared, be congenial with his own. He took occasion, therefore, to ask Hathbrand, his esquire, in the presence of lady Bertha, what he thought of the affair? "Hathbrand," cried he, in a lofty, but courteous tone, "do tell us what you know of this foolish old woman whom the country people call the hag? is she not a maniac?"

"There can be no doubt of it, my lord," answered the suppliant Hathbrand.

"Tell lady Bertha the stories which you have heard recounted of her."

Hathbrand was preparing a long recital.

"Do not," said the baron, whispering to him as lady Bertha walked towards the window, "do not say a word of the supernatural powers of this woman, lest it should alarm your lady's susceptible mind, I would have the impression of this disagreeable accident to wear away."

The assiduous Hathbrand took the hint at once, and recounted only those things which served to establish the opinion of the Hag's insanity, after which, the baron, having secured his point, cried out with a haughty tone, "For my own part, I think that this old wretch should be severely punished, and I shall give orders to the wardens of the forest to have her dragged hither."

"Alas! do not let me see her," cried the lady Bertha; "I am terrified sufficiently already, and tremble at the bare mention of her name; preserve me, blessed saints, from the conjurations of that wicked woman! but pray, my lord, exercise no vengeance upon her, lest the poor creature should indeed be mad, all that I wish, is the love and favour of my lord and husband, and I will be happy, notwithstanding the imprecation of the hag. It is not, after all, in the power of the wicked to oppose the will of Heaven."

The baron, with a countenance of concern and complacency, entreated the lady Bertha to compose her mind. "If it is your desire," cried he, "that the old witch——"

"Witch!" repeated the lady Bertha, "is she then a witch?"

"The foolish ignorant people call her so," replied the baron carelessly, though chagrined enough at the inadvertency of the expression, "but she is, in truth, only a poor childish old woman, who inhabits a hut on the heath, that no one would live in but herself."

"Well, my lord," answered the lady Bertha, "I thank you for your courtesy to me, and for your regard for my happiness, but unless we were sure that she spoke in malice, or from the wicked inspirations of the devil, let not this poor creature be molested. She may be mad, let her not, therefore, my lord, be molested."

The baron bowed his head, and looked at the obsequious Hathbrand, in a way so significant, that he understood it and withdrew.

The baron had now gained his point. The Hag was not to be disturbed, but he grew every day more and more restless in his mind on the subject of her visit, its motives, and the meaning of her malediction; he was superstitious enough to believe in the power of the spirits of darkness, because he trusted that those powers could bestow on their favourites the gifts of wealth, and of ambition. If, indeed, they had not been thought to possess those powers, he would perhaps have ridiculed the superstition, which on that account he permitted to enslave his mind. It was, it is true, mixed up with terrors of the future punishment of crimes, but the baron, whose mind was constantly occupied in plans of enjoyment, and security for the pleasure and ambition of this world, gave no time for the contemplation of the destinies which one day or other await the bad.

The child Edward, the son of the lady Bertha by her former lord, advanced hourly in beauty and comeliness; he was now about fifteen months old, and extremely engaging.

Nearly the whole of the time of the lady Bertha was taken up with her tender care of this infant, for she was a kind and affectionate mother, as well as a noble and accomplished lady.   It now happened, however, that the lady Bertha gave some promise of a child to her present lord, the baron, and which promise became daily strengthened by the appearance her shape evinced.

The baron de La Braunch, as it may be supposed, was well pleased at the possibility of its proving to be a male; for though the rich demesnes of the late lord of Martindale would descend to the child Edward, yet the baron thought it might happen that the child would die, and he being the next heir, in right of his lady, the whole fortunes of either house would descend to the promised offspring of his loins; such were at times the flattering, proud, and brilliant hopes, which occupied the mind of the baron, he managed nevertheless to govern his temper admirably towards the little Edward, nay, he even at times caressed the growing object of his hate.

CHAPTER VII

The domestics' account of the appearance of the witch,
with their reflections thereon.

THE appearance of the witch at the dinner had had a wonderful effect on all the servants, they would not any of them venture alone into the apartments, and their conjectures about the visit of the Hag were equally curious. They magnified her denunciation into a curse on the whole family, and each began already to discover in themselves the effects of her malice. Old Doric was the first to declare, that, by the measurement of his doublet, he was poisoned, and had increased sensibly many degrees in bulk; Jonas, too, felt extraordinary effects, and had, since the visit of the Hag, worn away in an equal ratio with the increase of his friend. The *maids* also felt uncommon symptoms, and each began to calculate on their approaching dissolution. Jonas, however had recourse to *spirits* to drive away the sorceress, which they did so very completely, that he was perfectly persuaded, by the time night arrived, that his fears were groundless, and that he enjoyed the same state of health as before. Nor was Doric without his means of consolation: he applied to the mathematics, and as he could not find any thing like the demonstration that the sides of a right-angled triangle are equal, in his mind, respecting the Hag's infernal qualifications, he established the proposition in his mind that she was actually mad; ergo, any body must be mad who thought her a witch, and that it did not require any conjurer to find out that she was only a poor old woman.

Notwithstanding, however, the self-reconciliations of these ingenious domestics, after the battle of their opinions in their own minds, they nevertheless, in their sober and thinking moments, used to dread the consequences of the Hag's interview at the castle; and these sentiments of consternation were daily kept up by the country-people at market, who never failed to produce evidence that very nearly shook the logic of old Doric himself.

CHAPTER VIII

The Birth of a Son.

THE time approached fast for the accouchement of the lady Bertha. The bugles sounded only the softest notes from the battlements, the drums were muffled, and the watch walked their rounds gently through the courts of the castle.

At length the time arrived.

One night the domestics of the castle were awakened, and their lady was safely delivered of a boy, to the unspeakable satisfaction of the baron.

The next day, the bugles sounded cheerfully from the turrets, and couriers were dispatched round the country, with the glad tidings, to the different knights who were in friendship with the baron. Nor was that proud lord neglectful of conveying the news to the king, which he did with his own hand.

The baron de La Braunch viewed this infant as the firm guarantee of his future good fortune in life; the more however, he reflected on this rising prospect of honour and of wealth, the more strong grew his enmity to the little Edward. Lady Bertha, on the other hand, was so rejoiced at the birth of an infant which promised to her the increased affection of her lord, that her assiduous regard for her former child became divided; she loved the little Edward still, yet the pretensions of that infant to the regards of its mother, were in part, superseded by a claim of a more immediate and necessary attention.

The baron de La Braunch already gave notice of the intended preparations for the christening of the infant, which event promised another day of festivity to the domestics at the castle, and to the numerous tenantry of the surrounding country.

CHAPTER IX

The Preparations for the Christening.

THE most officious and busy on this occasion, as well, indeed, as on all others, was old Doric, the steward, and purveyor of the castle; he rightly conjectured, that an increase of family would, by arithmetical progression, necessarily infer an increase of the stock of provisions; and he took care to lay in enough to have served the household for a month.

Ranetrude was not inactive; she was employed in preparing the splendid decorations of the bed of the infant, and the raiment in which it was to be clothed at the font.

Jonas was as much pleased with the promise of more festivity; to say the truth, he resisted every thing like dulness, or melancholy, and was never so happy, as when every body was so too.

CHAPTER X

The Christening.

The day of the christening at length arrived.

Numerous guests were invited.

Father Velaschi was sent for; the minstrels again prepared their harps for the songs of joy and festival, and the sumptuous board was again spread with the choicest delicacies.

The gates of the castle were thrown open, a train of knights and their ladies appeared, passing over each of the seven draw-bridges, but the baron had, on this occasion, more illustrious visitors than on the former. The prince Ethelred honoured him with his presence, and the princess Argalia, with the white hair, the most renowned beauty at court, had signified her intention of becoming one of the sponsors.

Father Velaschi arrived in time to perform the holy ceremony of baptism.

The most splendid entertainment was served up in the hall, on this occasion, and the baron and lady Bertha were seated as before, at the head of the table, where both of them did honour to their illustrious guests by their courtesy and attention.

The infant, wrapped up in a mantle of gold cloth, on which was the escutcheon of the baron, was shown to the company, and received the caresses of the princess Argalia, and of the other ladies, who were delighted with the opportunity of flattering the desires and ambition of the baron.

The hour of dinner passed over without any interruption of the harmony of the guests, and the news of the chapel having been lighted up for the ceremony, was received with general delight.

At length the party arose from the table, and the ladies, attended by their knights, passed through the long avenue from the hall of the castle to the oratory.

Three large wax-tapers, in golden candle-sticks, stood before the altar, and seven censers filled with burning frankincense, diffused their odoriferous perfumes.

CHAPTER XI

The Font.

FATHER Velaschi was employed in the holy preparations for the baptism, the vespers of the virgin Mary were repeated, and the hymn of the holy sacrament, *Corporis mysterium*, sung; the attendants were dispatched to bring the infant.

Some time had elapsed, when presently a horrid scream was heard.

Terror was in every face.

Opposite father Velaschi, at the font, stood a figure wrapped up in a dark mantle.

It held the infant in its arms, and, with a malicious grin, attempted to cross its forehead with the holy water.

It was the Hag.

The lady Bertha uttered a dreadful shriek, and fell prostrate on the floor of the chapel.

The baron advanced a few steps, but the witch, seizing the child by the arm, held it up in a menacing attitude, as if she would, on being interrupted, dash the innocent to the ground.

The baron, however, seized the arm of the witch.

The Hag resigned her prey.

It was delivered to the women.

Father Velaschi uttered a prayer. *Benedictus Deus.*

The baron with a stern voice demanded the reason of this second intrusion, and in his rage ordered the hag to be seized.

Several of the knights would have prevented her departure, but the witch placing her withered hand on the breast of Velaschi, the monk involuntarily gave way and suffered her to pass.

The Hag smiled, with a look of defiance that showed the whole of her one tooth, and mumbled to the baron, as she went forth;

"When thou hast need of the Hag, thou shalt seek her."

The baron revolved the sentence in his mind.

Father Velaschi was at prayers.

The lady Bertha was, with the attention of her attendants, restored to herself.

She had taken the infant in her own arms.

She wept over it.

The dreadful perturbation this accident had produced, prevented, for some time, the ceremony of baptism from taking place.

It was at length permitted to go on; Father Velaschi read the *Oremus*—he approached the font—he blessed the infant, which at the desire of the baron, was christened Hugo. The hymn, *Lucis Creator Optime*, was sung.

The guests returned to the supper-table, when the baron gave orders that the draw-bridges should be raised, that every stranger might be excluded. The night, therefore, passed without any further interruption, and the lady Bertha, as well as the whole company, were prevailed on to believe that the witch was mad.

CHAPTER XII

The reflections of the Baron on the Hag's second intrusion.

The next morning, the baron took an opportunity to ruminate alone, in his garden, on the remarkable words of the Hag;

"When thou hast need of the Hag, thou shalt seek her."

He considered the sentence of the witch, partly as an invitation, and knowing the wickedness of his own heart, began to think that he was a favourite of the witch, and that she would readily assist any mischievous design he might entertain, against the lady Bertha, or her child Edward, against whom his own dislike grew stronger every day, for he suffered all that misery of apprehension, which painted the probability of the child's living to succeed to the rich demesnes of his father, lord Edward of Martindale, now enjoyed by himself, in the right of his marriage with lady Bertha, and to which, in the case of the infant Edward's death, he and his offspring would succeed.

On the subject of the child Edward, therefore, the baron was ever restless and disturbed; he found that he could not altogether wean the affections of lady Bertha from that infant, delighted as she was with her second child, and desirous to show the offspring of her present lord every tender mark of maternal affection, yet she could not altogether forsake the little Edward, who was an engaging and sensible child, and the image of his father.

Now the baron de La Braunch, although bold in his carriage, and like a lion in the fight, was superstitious in the highest degree, and trembled at the thought of supernatural intelligence, which might inform him of bad fortune, though he longed to know the secrets of futurity; he could not account for, nor reconcile to himself, the second appearance of the Hag, and began to think that she must have meant something beyond what her words implied. In short, though an abject old woman was beneath even his contempt, yet, when that old wretch was believed to be a witch, he entertained some fears of her resentment, as well as a secret desire to know more of her.

The baron, therefore, took an opportunity, the next morning, to walk towards the heath; he was careful in making more particular inquiries concerning that extraordinary old woman, and found both his hopes and fears partly realized concerning her; it was told him that she was so wondrously skilled in magic, that she could divine every thing that would happen in future, to those who applied to her for information, and that her prediction never failed; that she could raise up the spirits of the departed, that she could give riches and honour to any on whom she pleased to bestow them, that she never forgave an insult, and that, having the power, by means of the fiend she worshipped, to torment and perplex, she could produce, by the power of her art, any accident of mischief or evil that she pleased.

The baron, on the recital of the capabilities of the witch, began to be sorry that he had treated her with so much harshness and contempt; yet, as he could not have done otherwise, from respect to lady Bertha, he reconciled that circumstance to his mind, and thought only how he could make her some atonement.

The baron entertained thoughts that the Hag might be useful to him, and he returned to the castle, occupied with schemes and fancies, apparently as wild, as they were in their design monstrous, and wicked. Among others, the most extraordinary that he proposed to himself, was a visit to the Hag, at her dwelling, that he might know more of her from herself, and judge of her potency in the art of magic.

CHAPTER XIII

The Illuminated Castle.

IN an almost impervious part of the forest, near a place known by the name of the Fell of Ravensworth, and close to the dwelling of

24

the Hag, stood an antient castle, almost entirely in ruins, and un-inhabited by any living creature, which indeed was partly owing to a tradition of its being frequented by devils, who held within its walls a nightly rendezvous, and partly to its being so near the dwelling of the witch.

This castle had formerly been inhabited by the family of La Braunch, but had been forsaken for a great many years, on account of its decay, and the superior accommodations of the other residence; it was not in the recollection of any person then living, that it had been occupied.

It was attested by numerous inhabitants of the villages adjoin-ing the heath, and those of the most discreet, and sober, that at night this castle became sometimes suddenly illuminated; that mu-sic was often heard at those times, and that, in an instant, the lights seen through the casement of the turrets would be extinguished, and every thing left again in total darkness.

No one of the villagers around would venture to develop this mystery. There was not any who would approach near enough, day or night, to convince their own senses, nor indeed could they very well reach the castle, as the way to it was overgrown with under-wood and no path whatever presented itself.

The baron, however, had formed frequent resolutions to him-self, of going to explore this antient dwelling of his ancestors; he might, indeed, have easily caused the ground to have been cleared, by the help of his numerous tenantry, but he had been always di-verted from that object by circumstances and events that more immediately claimed his attention.

It was now, however, that the baron began to think seriously of a visit to this deserted spot, where he thought that he might pos-sibly find some curious relics of his family. It was reported to con-tain a valuable gallery of old and curious arms, spears, and battle-axes, with the armour of its antient possessors.

The baron considered that he could include in his journey a visit to the Hag, whom his curiosity, and the answers he had re-ceived to his inquiries, made him more and more desirous to see. He therefore gave orders to his esquire, Hathbrand, to be in readi-ness to attend him, and chose the next evening for the purpose.

In the meantime the baron occupied himself in the considera-tion of the questions he would propose to the Hag; as ambition and riches were uppermost in the baron's mind, and the constant objects of his contemplation, it may be easily conjectured that his intended inquiries had that tendency.

The object of disgust to the baron, and the stumbling-block to his future greatness, was the little infant Edward. "Cruel circumstance," cried the baron, as he revolved the future probable events of his life in his mind, "cruel circumstance, that that little brat should, in a few more years, strip me and my house of its wealth and lustre; that a child of lord Edward of Martindale should dim the greatness of the family of La Braunch, and that my own offspring should be left poor and dependant. Wherefore," said he, "did I marry lady Bertha, but to obtain the splendour and advantages of wealth; I was not enamoured with her, I had no true regard. It was to answer the purpose of improving the fortunes of my antient house, that in my mind I consented to this alliance; I wished for the grandeur of riches, that I might display the habiliments and equipage of wealth, that I might have the notice of the king.—Yes, I will inquire, of the Hag, my future destinies—I will ask if the little urchin is to live; perhaps it is in the book of fate that the child may die soon; the poor little thing may go to heaven, and then the baron de La Braunch will be undisturbed in the enjoyment of his wealth and grandeur, yet may not this witch tell me something that may contradict those hopes? Yes, but my eager curiosity will not suffer me to remain in a state of uncertainty, when the information of which I stand in need for my happiness, may be so easily obtained.

The baron, indeed, could not dismiss the subject from his thoughts; and, though coward enough to dread the chance of a disappointment from the lips of the beldam, yet so strong was the desire of visiting her, that it obtained the ascendancy, and he was determined to risk the inquiry; his temper had become, of late, violently irritable, in consequence of these suggestions and fears working in his mind; for though the baron was always haughty, proud, and imperious, yet, as he disdained to speak at all to his vassals, they were but seldom troubled with his anger; almost every command was communicated through his esquire, Hathbrand, and he found it his interest to bear all the insulting irritations of his lord; he was always obsequious, and, as he never presumed to answer, the storm necessarily died away.

Lady Bertha was possessed of that mild dignity of character, which, though it had not obtained her the love of the baron, yet preserved her from incivility; indeed the baron was too accomplished a knight, to behave with rudeness to a lady, much more to a lady of rank; the strong workings of his mind, and of his passions, never betrayed him into any indecency of behaviour.

CHAPTER XIV

The Baron's first visit to the Hag.

IT was about the hour of seven in the evening, in the Autumn of the year, when the baron set out for the habitation of the witch; the broom on the heath was in full blossom, and its low heads formed a beautiful and picturesque landscape, which received a second tinge from the rays of the sun descending towards the horizon.

The baron de La Braunch, attended only by his esquire, Hathbrand, crossed the heath, and approached near the dwelling of the Hag; and hereabouts he thought proper to dismiss his companion; he did not, it is true, much relish the idea of an interview with this minister of the devil, alone, but he knew the wicked purposes of his heart, and the end he would effect by it; he knew that he dared not trust any living creature to be a witness to the conversation, and to the questions that he might demand of the witch.

It was almost dark, and the smoke from the hut of the witch ascended in a black column from the cavity made in the side of it from a chimney. The door, too, was open, and from thence also issued smoke, but of a lighter hue.

The baron had desired his attendant to wait about an hundred yards of the spot, under a pretext that he wished for an hour's solitary meditation in the forest.

When the baron approached nigh the door of the Hag's dwelling, he discovered her within, stooping over a large kettle, or cauldron, and stirring some materials with a stick. It was from this cauldron that the smoke issued; and, on the baron's entrance into the hut, he thought the vessel seemed to contain large pieces of human flesh; had not his heart been hardened by the frequency of his cruel imaginations, he would have shuddered at the sight; he did not feel, however, any sentiment of the kind, though an unaccountable dread of the supernatural intelligence of the witch took such hold on him, that he would gladly have withdrawn from the settled purpose of his heart, had he not been noticed by the witch, who had observed him and mumbled forth a welcome from her skinny lips, as she skimmed the broth from her kettle with a large wooden ladle which she held.

"Aye, aye," cried she as he approached, "I thought that you would come, well what is it you want with me?"

The baron attempted to answer her with all the courtesy he was master of, yet, the malignant smile of the witch, the sight of the cauldron, the wretchedness and misery of the place, the horrid appearance of the half-starved cat, thirsting as it were for blood, and screaming with hunger at his approach, the one-winged raven, altogether struck him with a panic of terror; a cold palsy seized his limbs, his majestic frame trembled, and he viewed the witch with a superstitious dread and horror.

The baron's first inquiry of the Hag was the way to the castle in the wood.

"I would go thither, Hag," cried he, "thou canst direct me to the path."

"Thou mayst spare thyself the trouble of that visit," replied the Hag, "its turrets are all that thou wilt be able to see of it, the path to it has for these many years been choaked up by the growth of brushwood and underwood; besides, what wouldst thou do there? none venture near it, it hath evil spirits haunt it."

"And with such," replied the baron, "thou art, Hag, unless report belies thee, well acquainted; but fear not me, I will not disturb thee, Hag—thou shalt have my protection."

"Rather say that thou needest mine," answered the witch.

"Thine!!"

"Mine, baron; I know the purposes of thy heart, and am prepared to serve thee."

"Art thou indeed?"

"Yes—but thou wilt not favour the poor Hag."

"By the——"

"Beware of oaths——No——thou didst command that I should leave thy presence."

"Why didst thou choose, then, so untimely a visit—And then thy imprecation."

"It will happen."

"Lady Bertha——"

"Will be wretched."

"Show me, Hag, these things."

"What wouldst thou give to know them?"

"Ask what thou wilt, of money or favour; thou shalt have rich gifts from my munificence, show but the secrets of futurity."

"I want not riches."

"What is it, then, Hag, that thou wouldst have?"

The Hag paused.

"Say," repeated the baron.

"Blood!" was the answer of the Hag.

"Blood!!!"

"The food of mischief, of calamity, of agony, of distress."

"Execrable wretch!" (exclaimed the baron aside)—"Well, Hag, show me some specimens of thine art, produce me, if thou canst do it, one of the powers of darkness whom thou servest. Show me the treasures of the world, how to attain, and keep them; convince me that thou canst gratify the vast appetite of my ambition—and then thou shalt not want for food—show me now—I come prepared for horrors."

"Another time," answered the Hag, "at present I am busy; when thou next comest, I will unfold to thee the secrets of my art, but thou must be stout."

"Fear not me," returned the baron.

"Well, then, visit me," replied the Hag, "when the moon shall have made her conjunction with the planet Saturn. It is but a few days to wait for that configuration—Come to me when the high tide of mischief is up—When the fiery vapours dance along the ground at midnight—When the envenomed toad is lighted by the glow-worm, to its damp chamber, beneath the leaves of the purple violet—Then the time will be near, the spectres will abound upon the earth, the demons and fiends will be active, strong, and numerous, and alert in mischief, then mayst thou hope for the accomplishment of the wishes of thine heart."

"I will attend thee, Hag," returned the baron.

"Be it so."

Immediately a thick cloud of black and noisome smoke ascended, and filled the cabin—The Hag was lost to the sight of the baron, and it was with difficulty that he found the door, although it was in his reach; he was in the open air again; he crossed the heath, towards the spot where he had left Hathbrand, he looked round about him; he saw no one; yet he fancied that he saw shades, which flitted past him, and were lost in the high broom that grew on the common; he felt terror, but a malicious satisfaction filled his breast; he halloed Hathbrand; a voice answered; it was his esquire.

"It is dark," cried the baron, "let us go to the castle."

"Very dark," replied Hathbrand.

There were some remains of terror in the face of the baron.

The moon, now and then, burst from behind the huge black clouds, that travelled swiftly by, and indicated the approach of a storm.

They travelled onwards; the castle appeared at a distance.

During this absence of the baron, the lady Bertha was engaged, watching over her infants; it was late, she was low in spirits; she looked at her children, and sighed; she kissed first the infant Edward; she thought first of poor Edward who had not a father, and then she kissed Hugo; she sung them to sleep, it was with a ballad.

> The wind blew high, the night was dark,
> As yet appear'd no cheering ray,
> The seamen of the shipwreck'd bark
> Despairing wait th' approach of day.
>
> Poor Mary views, with frantic eye,
> While the black clouds the sky deform,
> Rent sails and tackling, drifting nigh,
> The horrid trophies of the storm.
> And now, with cruel doubts opprest
> She sees one brave the billow's roar;
> She runs to clasp him to her breast,
> It was Edward reach'd the shore.

The bugle sounded; the watch-word was given and the draw-bridges raised; the baron entered. The lady Bertha tried to recover her spirits; she could not—she received him with a heavy heart. She seemed to have some supernatural evidence pressing on her mind, of the baron's having been in some mysterious danger. The baron retired to rest, thoughtful and gloomy.

After the visit the baron had made to the witch, he grew sullen and reserved, his time was usually passed in his library, or in parading, for hours, the turrets of his castle; he now gave a loose to the imaginations of his heart, and dwelt incessantly on the great object of his anxiety, the secure possession and enjoyment of the wealth he had in prospect, which would place him on an equality with princes; he knew that expedients must be used; he knew that the Hag only could help him; that she would readily do it, from the natural enmity she had to the good; he only hoped that she was equal in wickedness to his purpose, for he had contemplated the past events and actions of his life, and he preferred the agression of successful crimes, that might lead to the accomplishment of his hopes, to the sad work of repentance, when enjoyment was so near at hand.

The baron was in this mood one day when the little Edward came lisping to his knees; the baron stampt, the infant fell to the ground; the baron recollected himself, took it in his arms, fondled it, and gave it to the attendant who was by; "I was in thought," cried the baron, "poor little wretch, take it hence."

CHAPTER XV

The Condition of lady Bertha.

LADY Bertha, who was altogether unsuspicious of any change in the baron, must have been insensible, if she had not noticed the gloom that hung over the brow of her lord; yet she was sufficiently discreet not to interfere with the subject of his thoughts. She did indeed, one day, ask if any thing had happened to cause him uneasiness, but the answer he gave her was, such, as to prevent any further questions, and she was too obedient to his humour, to press a subject that was disagreeable.

The baron de La Braunch, though he began now evidently to neglect his notice of the child Edward, yet caressed his own infant with all the becoming tenderness of a parent. This circumstance of affection, in a great measure, eased the mind of lady Bertha; she gathered from thence, that the baron still loved her, and that he would continue to do so, while that little pledge of their regard was in existence. She was, besides, happy in the attachment and obedience of her domestics, who adored their mistress; Ranetrude, who was a sensible and lively companion, would not suffer her mistress to despond, nor permit any little circumstance of the barons irritability of temper to press on her mind, she amused her as much as lay in her power by her pleasant discourse, entertaining stories, and the ballads she had learnt, and could sing with sweetness and melody. These endeavours of the hand maid of lady Bertha to amuse, were kindly accepted.

The little Edward was the favourite of old Doric and Jonas. The first persuaded himself that he would come to be a great mathamatician; that he should have, some day or other, the pleasure of teaching him how to solve a problem, and of making him comprehend the elements of Euclid. Old Jonas was delighted, on the other hand, with the childs regard for a drop of Rhenish, with which by the bye the old butler never failed to supply him slily, when out of the sight of his lady mother, and of the attendants. On these occasions Jonas used to place the boy on his knee, and sensible in his mind that wine was good for every thing, and for every body, he used to pour it down its throat until it went fast asleep in his arms, by which consequence the servants used to say that the little Edward was never so happy and quiet as with old Jonas.

The baron de La Braunch used to pass the greater part of his time in hunting. The truth was, that he wished to amuse away the interval of time which had to come before the day of his visit to the Hag, for which he was very eager. He had fixed his mind on prying into the vast volume of futurity, and wished to know even the bad, as well as good, which awaited him; he had, too, seen the monster, and had become acquainted with her blood-stained thoughts, he had no longer a doubt of her supernatural powers, her dwelling, her appearance, her language, altogether proved her to be a witch, he was flattered by his superstition, since he believed that the powers of darkness had the gifts at will to bestow, for which he longed with so insatiate an appetite. It was not the baron's disposition to look further than to the enjoyments of this life.

CHAPTER XVI

The Baron's second visit to the Hag.

THE time approached for the baron's second visit to the Hag—he had attended carefully to the signs. The day arrived; the hour; it was about the rising of the moon.

The evening was gloomy; a mist overspread the heath, and the setting sun had left no gleam as the promise of its return.

The lady Bertha was low, and disturbed in mind. She had not slept the night before; her rest had been broken by frightful dreams. She dreamed that the baron stabbed her to the heart. She screamed and awoke: "What," said she to herself, "could make me dream any thing so horrid! the baron loves me, and treats me with respect; dreams are idle things, and it is wrong to brood over them." Such were the wise reflections of lady Bertha, and it was not until the baron retired for the evening, that she grew melancholy.

The good have always a remedy on these occasions; she flew to prayer, and to practise those duties which are always pleasing to the Deity, the duties of a tender and affectionate mother; she had forsaken her fears as ungrateful to Providence.

The baron left the castle, attended only by his esquire. He used the same precautions as before. When he approached the hut, he desired that he might proceed alone.

The baron observed a light in the hovel: it was only the glimmer of a fire, which, every now and then, flashed and disappeared. He lifted up the latch, and entered.

He found the Hag alone; she was seated on the three-legged stool, by the fire-side.

It was a considerable time before she spoke.

The cat mewed, and walked slowly round the room.

The raven flapped his long wing.

The Hag sat doubled, with her lips chattering, and her mouth working.

She seemed busy in some conjurations.

The baron stood with his arms folded, observing her.

He addressed her.

The Hag answered not a word.

He addressed her again.

She made no reply.

He addressed her the third time.

At length she looked him full in the face; "So you are punctual."

"I am ever so," replied the baron.

"Yes, I know, when great lords want any thing they *can* be punctual."

"Thou art out of temper, Hag."

"It is my way at times; thou must not be offended. I have to deal with fiends, and devils; and sometimes they cross and vex me. I am but a servant."

"Is it a fit time for our purpose?"

"No. It is too soon: the gloom of night, the time of vapours must first come on. Nothing is yet abroad but what is wholesome. You are too eager, sir; but it is ever so. The most unruly of the devil's subjects is man."

The Hag arose; she tottered to one corner of the hut where was a bundle of wood.

She drew forth a ragged splinter; she put it into the fire. The point of the splinter kindled into a flame; she lighted with it the wick of an iron lamp, that stood on the floor. She seated herself again.

"Is it yet dark?" cried the Hag.

The baron looked from the door. The gloom of night had come on.

"It is dark," answered the baron.

The Hag arose.

"Now, then, we will begin our work. Are you staunch?" cried the witch.

"I disdain fear," replied the baron.

"Aye, aye, it is mighty well," replied the witch; "it is mighty well; it is mighty well."

The baron was bold; but the grim visage of the Hag illumined only by the pale glimmer of the lamp, struck him with disgust and horror.

"Are you ready," cried the witch, "to witness the terrors of this night?"

"I am prepared," answered the baron.

"Now, then, follow me," cried the witch, holding the iron lamp in her hand. "Follow."

"Whither?"

"No matter; thou needst not fear. Thou art under the protection of the Hag."

"I can defend myself from harm," cried the baron, drawing a massy sword from his side.

"Ha, ha, you are wonderfully bold," cried the Hag, with a short convulsive laugh, "you are wonderfully bold; but you will see none but friends."

"I am ready to follow thee; lead the way."

At these words the Hag stamped with her foot; a thick smoke filled the hut.

She stamped a second time. The baron fixed his eyes attentively upon her.

The Hag stamped a third time. The space of the cabin was filled with flame: it encircled the witch.

"You must throw this mantle over your face," cried the Hag to the baron, as he stood in wonder as to what was to follow. "Fear not," reiterated the Hag.

The baron permitted the mantle to be thrown over him. He found himself led by the corner of his cloak, which the Hag had gathered into her hand. He was led about twenty paces. A dismal groan was heard as he moved forward: he desired to see whither he was going; and refused to proceed further.

The mantle was removed from before the face of the baron, when he found himself in the midst of a vaulted chamber, without any other light than that in the hand of the witch.

In exploring every avenue and recess of this dreary place, the baron beheld only gloom and darkness.

The Hag placed the lamp on the ground.

The baron's eyes were fixed upon a dark recess in the chamber, from whence he had heard proceed a dismal moan. He beheld a stupendous object arise! It was mishapen, but had something of the appearance of a human being. It was huge in form, its body black, and its face jaundiced, and smeared with blood. It roared, as it arose, like a lion which is roused from its den.

The baron startled at this object of terror; but how was his horror increased, when he saw that the monster held in one hand a javelin imbrued in human gore, and in the other a cup full of blood, and which it hugged close to its bosom.

A distant scream now reverberated through the chamber, at which the spectre started into a recess of the vault, and was seen no more.

"What was this?" cried the baron, the hair of his head standing on end.

"A demon," answered the Hag.

"His name?"

"Ugall."

"His purpose?"

"To inspirit the murderer."

"Ha!" repeated the baron.

"Art thou satisfied of my power? Wouldst thou see more, or wouldst thou spare thyself the rest?"

"I would see more; show me the spirit of the dead."

"Whose spirit wouldst thou see?"

"I would," cried the baron, with a haughty and contemptuous sneer, "see the spirit of Harold."

"Of Harold! Why of Harold! I will convince thee better of my power. The baron forgets that he knows not the figure of Harold. I will show thee the spirit of one whose figure thou knowest."

"Proceed," replied the baron.

All was still in the chamber. The Hag drew a circle three times round the lamp, which gave a pale and dismal light. She muttered some unintelligible words.

The baron watched the Hag attentively.

At length from a corner of the vault glided a figure; it seemed formed only of transparent ether. It was not Harold. It was the form of a female, with a light robe thrown over her: her features were angelic though pale. It carried a cup in one hand; it waved the other to the baron.

For an instant he stood aghast!

"Hide me," cried he, dreadfully convulsed, "hide me from that horrid sight! Deceitful Hag, is this the spirit that I would have seen!"

As he spoke the spectre retired.

"I have seen enough," cried the baron.

"And you acknowledge the power of my art?"

"I do."

"Yes, yes; the Hag thought that she could see thee."

"We will return then," cried the Hag, throwing the mantle over him.

They trod some paces; the Hag withdrew the mantle; they were together in the hut.

The baron supported himself, with his arm against the rugged wall. The Hag had seated herself on the three-legged stool.

The baron was wrapt up in meditation. He was sick with horrors; but he was pleased and gratified with the power of his agent; he was willing to become a servant of the fiend's, that he might be the highest among men. Yet he had not recovered from the panic which the supernatural powers of the witch had produced.

The Hag spoke. "Baron I know thy thoughts; I know the machinations of thy heart; thy wishes, thy hopes, and thy fears. I have shown thee more than thou didst expect, that thou mightest be satisfied of my skill. Now then command me; but I must be richly paid."

"I will not be ungrateful: what is the price?"

"Shall I have it?"

"Thou shalt."

"Swear it. Swear by hell."

"I swear; by hell."

"Bring me, then, the child."

"Ha! Say what child?"

"Lady Bertha's."

"Which of them?"

"I care not which, so it is lady Bertha's."

The baron's countenance brightened at this explanation; for there was an infant that he would willingly have exposed to all the horrors of the event.

"And what wouldst thou do with the babe?" inquired the baron.

"Trouble not thyself, baron; bring it me to-morrow: thou hast sworn. It must be done to-morrow."

As she spoke these words, the Hag laughed. It was an hysteric laugh.

"Now baron," cried the Hag, "what are thy thoughts, thy hopes? Thus devils gratify each other. The offerings they make are human beings. Riches and honours shall be thine; let us be friends; give me thine hand."

As she spoke, the hag put forth her shrivelled palm.

Unwillingly the baron touched the palsied and venomous fingers of the witch.

"May I depend on this thy present?"

"Depend on me," replied the baron.

"Aye, and then I will take thee where the power resides, that can give thee wealth, and honours, and fame. That can harm and destroy, and make thee busy and bold in mischief. That can gratify thy desires, thy lusts, thy ambition, ha, ha, ha; we will have fine sport: we will whip and scourge the silly, mild, and humane, with calamity in plenty; we will mortify, and disappoint, and plague, and tease, aye, that we will: it will be fine sport."

Then the Hag began a song, with all the horrid gestures of fury; the notes were shrill and loud; her eyes glistened; she danced with her feet, and seemed drunk with the ecstasy of her thoughts.

"Farewel, Hag," cried the baron, "the infant Edward shall be thine."

"Thanks, noble baron," replied the Hag, with a horrid grin. "Farewel——to-morrow."

"To-morrow."

Thus ended the discourse between the baron de La Braunch and the witch of Ravensworth.

The baron returned towards the castle, across the heath; his mind occupied with the dreadful images he had beheld, in agony and misery, blended with the delightful promises which flattered his ambition.

CHAPTER XVII

The Baron's return to the Castle.

THE baron de La Braunch withdrew to his chamber the instant he entered its gates.

He desired that he might not be interrupted, and threw himself on a couch beneath the rich canopy in the audience-chamber, which was used for state occasions: his thoughts were engaged with the consideration of the homage, and respect, which would be paid him, the instant he should be in possession of the wealth of the boy Edward, and which would be sufficient to place him on a footing with princes, or to obtain, from the consequence it would give him in the realm, additional rank and honours from the king; he saw that by the cruel offering he was about to make his views would be realized. The child would doubtless be immolated; it would be presented as a sacrifice to the fiend; and then, the wealth and principalities of lord Edward would be his. But how to manage this diabolical plan so secretly, that lady Bertha should have no knowledge how the infant had been disposed of; how to reconcile her to its mysterious disappearance, in case that event could be brought about; how to soothe her into silence, and peace, were masterpieces of art, that required his most exquisite workmanship, yet, so vast, to him, was the object in view, that, with all the temerity of a bold and desperate mind, he determined on putting his design in execution.

CHAPTER XVIII

The Baron presents the Infant Edward an offering to the Hag.

THE next day, the baron, who had arranged every circumstance in his mind, appeared to lady Bertha with a face of unusual kindness, and complacency; not only to lady Bertha, but to his domestics. Nay, he had even address enough to caress, on that day, the little innocent which was his intended victim; and more, in conversation with lady Bertha, and her woman, Ranetrude, to plan out to its fond mother the future management and education of the child; the course of its studies; its future fortunes; its initiation into chivalry; its introduction to the king.

The lady Bertha, sensible of every word of kindness and of tenderness, pressed the babe to her bosom. It is true, she heaved an involuntary sigh.

The evening had come, and the glorious sun had withdrawn its gladdening presence from the castle.

The attendants of lady Bertha had taken their young lord, Edward, to rest; his mother had said her prayers over its little form, as it lay fast bound in refreshing sleep. The apartment where the child reposed, was next to lady Bertha's, and not any came near it, but herself and the most confidential of her women, nor could any pass into it, but through her own chamber. The baron, who frequently slept in his own room, went early to his chamber, and desired that he might not be disturbed; he complained of being ill, and that he wanted repose.

The lady Bertha reposed on her own bed.

Ranetrude, who slept with the infant, usually retired at an hour later than her mistress; the duties of her situation required some few arrangements previous to her going to her chamber; not any of the domestics had yet retired.

The baron, watching a fit opportunity, stole gently from his own room into lady Bertha's chamber; he observed that she was asleep; the infant Hugo lay at her breast; he found that she was not disturbed, and passed on, gently, into the chamber wherein the infant Edward slept; all was still. The child lay with its hands clasped, in an attitude of prayer. It was in a sweet and composed sleep.

The baron put down the light; he walked backwards and forwards; he listened; he paused: There was no further time to lose.

The moment suited: he put his hand underneath the mantle on which the child was laid, he raised the poor infant to his bosom, and, covering it with his cloak, crept gently through the chamber wherein reposed lady Bertha—he had taken the taper in his hand. As he passed by, he heard her moan; the rest of lady Bertha was disturbed, but she was unconscious of the theft of her beloved child.

The baron, who had taken care to make fast his door, listened for an instant, fearing even the approach of one of his own servants. He walked gently, the length of the gallery; all was silent; he descended the stairs.

There was a secret and subterraneous passage beneath the foundations of the castle; none had passed through for years; the key had always been in the possession of the baron; the passage led to the heath.

The baron, as he descended, felt the chilly moisture; the taper which he held, lengthened its blue flame, and quivered in the damp air; he proceeded some steps further, and came to the subterraneous passage, which narrowed as he went on. The child slept the whole time.

The baron paced on briskly; he thought that he heard voices behind, and his imagination presented before him the foul spectre, with the javelin, and the bowl of blood; now he fancied that some one was treading briskly after him, along the avenue, but he was more afraid of detection, or of disappointment in his plan, than of spirits.

At length the baron arrived at the iron door, which, concealed beneath the furze and underwood of the covered part of the heath, was unseen by the passenger, and unknown to any of the neighbouring villagers.

The baron only knew of such an ascent; he laid the infant gently on the moist earth; he placed the key within the jaws of the rusty lock; it would not stir. The baron had begun to think that all his labour and contrivance had been in vain; by a strong effort it turned. He unlocked the trap, but the rusty bolts which had become fixed were yet untried; nothing but the gigantic strength of the baron could have moved them; that, however, prevailed, and the heath appeared above.

The infant, which had been roused by the reverberating sounds occasioned by forcing the bolts, awoke, and began to cry. The baron endeavoured to hush the child, by every note of tenderness, and by every gentle caress; he put the half slumbering infant to his bosom; it thought that it was in its mother's arms, and was still.

The baron ascended for the few steps that led to the trap, and pushed it back with his hands, but could find no space large enough to get through the furze, which grew up to the entrance. This was a new difficulty, but when once set on mischief, the bad, who are always impatient, are not to be easily disturbed.

The baron was not to be impeded by obstacles; he placed his shoulder against the stems of the young saplings, and, treading the brushwood and brambles beneath his feet, forced his way through, to the open part of the heath, but not without his limbs being torn in the contest.

At length the baron found himself in a valley, which he knew to be beyond a branch of the river Eden, under the bed of which was the subterraneous passage. Here he stopt an instant, to muffle himself up in his cloak, and then, quickening his pace, went on, by the most secret winding paths, towards the heath.

In the way, the travellers met with but one solitary passenger, a man who was laden with a bundle of faggots on his back, tied round with a withy. As they passed, the child set up a cry, and the countryman called in a surly tone to the baron to know who and what he was, and what he did out with an infant at such a time; for the night had begun to be stormy, and gusts of wind and rain intercepted the way of the passenger. The baron made no reply, but hastened his steps; the countryman passed on.

The baron could discern the solitary hovel, in which dwelt the Hag, at a distance, by a pale glimmer of light from the window. He hastened his steps; he arrived at the door of the hut; he halloed, and the witch appeared at the entrance. The eyes of the Hag sparkled, as he approached; she said she had been expecting him; she looked with a malicious smile under his cloak; she chuckled at the sight.

The baron presented the child to the Hag. She took it within the grasp of her meagre hooked fingers, as a spider encloses in its fangs the helpless fly.

She laid the infant on the red flooring; in one corner of the hut lay a large knife, which she gathered up in one hand; she mumbled some sentences to herself; the baron stood still, observing every action of the witch.

The infant awoke at this instant, and, fixing its little eyes on the foul and deformed figure of the witch, uttered a piercing cry. It was a cry of terror. The witch was employed sharpening the knife on the floor; she took no notice of the crying child. The baron was agitated; he asked if his presence was longer necessary.

"Doubtless," answered the Hag, "dost thou not know that thou must work thy way to the favour of the fiend Askar, the prince of darkness, whom we worship: thou must use thyself to scenes of blood; thou must become familiar with horrors, they must be thy pastime, thy amusement." The baron was silent; the Hag stooped down; she lifted up the large-bladed knife; she took hold of the arm of the child; she pointed the knife downwards to its breast.

In an instant a luminous appearance, like a cloud of flame, filled the hut; a rushing noise was heard; the Hag trembled, from the taper ends of her long fingers, down even to her toes. She sunk by degrees to the ground; the knife fell from her withered fingers; she lay prostrate on her face, making the most hideous howlings, and convulsed in every limb; she was entranced.

The baron stood aghast, lost in wonder and horror, at the sudden affection which disturbed the witch; at length the Hag recovered by degrees.

She took a small piece of broken stone, in the shape of a triangle, from a corner of the hut—she placed it carefully in the centre of the floor; she gathered some live embers from the hearth; she drew some cabalistic characters on the stone with the fore finger of her right hand; she threw down the embers; she knelt down; she blew the embers away gently; she clapped her hands, as with joy; she arose; she took the child in one hand, and the knife in the other. She danced with the infant in her arms, and then, with the most frantic gestures, ran three times round the hut.

The baron paused—he wondered what would follow: the Hag was incensed; the infant screamed, and the third time the Hag disappeared with it in her arms. All was silent as death. The baron was left alone; he meditated on the event; there was not a whisper heard.

Two, three, four, five minutes, had elapsed; at length the Hag appeared before him; there was no child: the large-bladed knife was bloody. The Hag seated herself on the three-legged stool; she was silent.

"Wretch," cried the baron, (with an excellent dissimulation) "what is it thou hast done? the knife is bloody—Is it murdered then?"

"It is."

"And is it for this, that I have brought the infant to thee?" cried the baron.

"Hypocrite," replied the witch, "thou well deservest the regards of Askar!—didst thou not see how I was tormented; I would have had this choice morsel to myself; but the power of Askar overcame me, *I* have most reason to complain, *I* am robbed by the greedy fiend, robbed of my prey, not a finger of it has the Hag been allowed to touch; not even the thumb of the left hand—thou and he are both served, and I—I, the instrument of thy convenience, and of his pleasure, am disappointed; well, no matter, I dare not grumble in his presence; but I must have mischief—I am famished—I will have my glut."

The baron having gained his point, would now have willingly departed; wicked and hardened as he was, he had had his fill of horrors. He desired to depart, that he might give perfection to his villainy, by soothing the lady Bertha, and reconciling her to her loss.

The Hag was not disposed to let the baron go. "Thou art now," said she, "a servant of the mighty Askar. On the fourteenth day of the ensuing month, our sacrifice is held, at which the mighty Askar himself presides. If thou wouldst be lucky; if thou wouldst be rich; if thou wouldst have all the wealth and pleasures of the world, thou must be there. I will be thy conductor. Then will be the time to ask and to have; he will doubtless heap his favours on thee."

"I will come," answered the baron.

"Aye, thou wilt come, and see our midnight festivals; our games; our sports. Then will be the time for thy courage to be tried; thou must not then be woman-hearted. Well, well; go home, and try to comfort poor lady Bertha; she will suspect the Hag; thou wilt do well to gratify her resentment: cause me to be brought before thee; there is no proof against me, I shall be acquitted."

"Even so; I thank thee for this," answered the baron, "all will then end in conjecture. Farewel."

The baron left the hut.

It blew a tempest: the rain swept, in torrents, the heath.

43

The baron walked forward,—he approved the storm; it was not likely that any would be abroad to notice him.

It lightened;—horrid images, of various fanciful forms, flitted by, or danced along the heath before him!

He heard the wolf. He heard the wild cat.

The baron arrived at an empty hovel, he sought an indifferent shelter beneath its roof.

He beheld a white figure rise from a corner of the hovel! It was a white heifer, which had sheltered in the same place.

"Ideot that I am," cried the baron, "to be afraid of spirits; have I not been used to horrors! and bad spirits will not harm the man who seeks their assistance."

It lightened. The thunder roared immediately over the head of the baron; he saw the heavens open, with the convulsion of the storm, and emit liquid sheets of flame.

The baron hesitated his steps; he was even yet undaunted; he had been practised in greater horrors. He knew even of the mysteries of hell.

Presently the castle of La Braunch presented its turrets, through the obscurity of the tempest.

The baron had to seek for the entrance to the subterraneous passage; it was with difficulty that he found it. He had left the trap a little open; he entered, and closed it after him.

The lamp which he had left was yet burning.

He stopt in the middle of the passage, to consider for an instant, how he could best make his way to the chamber without being seen.

He sat down on the steps which led to the private stairs of the gallery, to listen; all was still.

"All will be well," cried the baron, "the great difficulty is disposed of: the brat is destroyed. I have only to act a little, and the affair will pass off as a shadow. The horrid mystery will never be discovered."

The baron ascended the private stairs, and entered the gallery where was his room. He had the taper in his hand.

If he had been seen, by any of the domestics, they would not have dared to ask him questions.

He retired, not to rest, but to suffer perturbations of mind, the conflicts of ambition and remorse.

CHAPTER XIX

The agony of Lady Bertha at the loss of her Infant.
The trial of the Hag.

THE attendants of lady Bertha had no sooner missed the child Edward, than they began to make the most busy and anxious inquiries. Ranetrude was the first who made the fatal discovery; she had entered the chamber of her mistress, and had passed through to prepare herself for rest; she looked at the bed for the child, and missed its little form which lay usually in one place. She imagined that lady Bertha had removed it to her own side. She approached the bed of her mistress, and found her asleep; the infant Hugo at her bosom, but little Edward was not there. Lady Bertha awoke; she inquired what was the matter. Ranetrude inquired for the child. "It sleeps," replied lady Bertha, "it is in its bed;" "Not so, my lady," answered Ranetrude, "the child is not there."

The lady Bertha arose hastily from the bed on which she had reposed. She sought the infant in the adjoining chamber; it was not there. The attendants were now summoned, and Ranetrude began to make the most busy and anxious inquiries; every servant was asked, if they had seen, or if they knew any thing of their young lord Edward.

Not any could afford the desired intelligence; and in the countenance of every domestic, were to be noticed evident marks of doubt and surprise. Difficult was the task of returning with the news that the child was no where to be found, and this they did repeatedly, after the renewed searches they made.

The child was missing. The unhappy lady Bertha received this distressing intelligence, with all the agony of a tender mother. The horrid sentence of the Hag, *Misery to the bride,* rushed upon her recollection, and she fainted away in the arms of her attendants.

It was needless to go to the baron's room; they were satisfied that the child could not be there; and after the command he had given, not to be disturbed, no one dared acquaint him with the accident which had happened. All was confusion and distraction.

The baron heard, from his chamber, a rumour of the distress, of which he too well knew the cause, and was wrapped up in contemplation on the passing events; his mind was too savage and ferocious to lament the death of the poor infant; all his thoughts were engaged on the success of the plan, which had so secretly and effectually put an end to the baneful object between him and his towering ambition. It is true, that sometimes he trembled at the reproaches of his conscience, and reflected that from all he had read in history, the wicked were in the end deserted by their guardian devils; however, this was remote, and the long wished-for hour of riches and honours was arrived. The baron trusted in the power, and supernatural aid of the witch of Ravensworth, to protect him from the adversities of this world, and did not look further.

At length the baron de La Braunch, glutted with success in his horrid plan, and full of the prospect of enjoyment of all he valued, considered that he could not have a better opportunity to exercise the plausibility of which he was so complete a master, than in the confusion which then reigned in the castle. He therefore arose, and descended to the chamber of the lady Bertha, prepared to meet, with coolness and affected ignorance, the history of the misfortune.

Lady Bertha, as soon as the baron entered the chamber, threw herself at his feet, and taking his hand in hers bathed it in tears: she related the horrid story of the infant Edward's being taken from the castle, and the ineffectual search which had been made, in all the colours which a frantic mother could give to such an event.

The baron, a complete master in dissimulation, stood as it were petrified with astonishment. For a minute he uttered not a syllable, but appeared enwrapt in consternation; at length he stamped his foot on the ground, and, in a voice that made an echo through the castle, demanded who had that night entered the castle.

The obsequious Hathbrand, Doric, Jonas, the porters, the guards, were all of them separately examined, but no one of them had seen a stranger enter.

The lady Bertha, in her agony and affliction, now first mentioned her suspicions of the Hag. The baron started.

"But why the Hag?" cried he.

"Her horrid curse," answered the lady Bertha, "has never been absent from my mind."

"True! it was remarkable; wretched beldam; yes; it shall be so."

The baron recalled his attendants, and gave instant orders that Hathbrand, and six chosen vassals, should instantly seek the witch, take her into custody, and at the same time explore her cabin, that they might find the infant, if it were there concealed.

The lady Bertha's face brightened with hope at this command. She fancied that she should see her child once again, and expressed a grateful acknowledgment of sensibility for the gallant conduct of the baron on the occasion.

CHAPTER XX

The trial of the Hag in the Audience-chamber.

MANY hours had not elapsed, before the sound of the trumpet announced the arrival of strangers: they were Hathbrand, and his followers, with the Hag in custody.

Lady Bertha was looking out with eagerness, and with frantic despair and hope. There was no infant.

The domestics of the castle shouted with joy, when they saw the Hag brought into the castle. The lady Bertha was disappointed, and sorrow was in her face, yet she hoped that some intelligence might be extorted from the witch.

The baron and lady Bertha ascended the throne of justice, in the audience-chamber. The Hag stood before them.

The baron sternly demanded, "If she recollected her intrusions at the castle, and the expressions which had come from her lips?"

The witch answered, with a malignant smile, "Yes."

"We have strong suspicions," said the baron, "that the misfortune which has happened in the castle has been brought about, Hag, by thy wicked art and contrivance; and the sentences which, at thy unwelcome visits, came from thy lips, amount almost to proof against thee."

"What have I done?" cried the Hag, "what is the matter now? always accusation, always unwarranted criminations against the Hag!"

"Dost thou know any thing? answer me directly and truly," cried the baron. "Dost thou know any thing of the infant lord Edward, who is missing from the castle?"

"No:" answered the witch. "What, is it lost? Truly you take great care of your cherubs! where were the attendants? where the mother? why am I to be accused? who saw me? why hadst thou not brought the pretty baby to the Hag? she would have nursed it carefully: sweet poppet! It was doubtless taken away by fairies."

As she uttered these words, the Hag showed a malicious grin on her face, that made the unhappy lady Bertha shudder with horror. She could not discover whether the witch was guilty of the theft, or whether her taunts were the reproaches of a mind angered at being falsely accused. She only heaved a heavy sigh.

The baron, as it might be expected, pretended to find the proofs insufficient to the charge against the witch; he appeared to the lady Bertha herself, who answered, "Heaven forbid that I should ask for punishment, where there may be the most slender chance of innocence. Pray let the Hag go." The witch retired; and, as she left the audience-chamber, murmured some unintelligible jargon, and burst out with a convulsive laugh.

The baron studiously endeavoured to console the lady Bertha, and to divert her attention from the object of her thoughts, to the care of the infant Hugo, the most likely method for him to succeed; in addition to which he constantly gave her hopes that the child was yet alive, and taken care of by some persons unknown, as otherwise if it had been their intention to have destroyed it, they could have effected their purpose without taking it from the castle.

CHAPTER XXI

An interval of some years.

TIME, which engaged the mind to fresh objects and pursuits, might have acted with like effect on the lady Bertha's disposition, had not the chaste and gentle deportments of that lady, prevented her from seeking consolation from amusement: her only relief and consolation was derived from her attentions to the child Hugo, and in observing the gradual progress of its understanding. This in some measure obliterated from her recollection the loss of her other infant. Her duty to the baron also, and her studious attentions to his will, kept her constantly engaged. She was never at ease but when employed in her domestic duties; and was never seen to smile, but when it was with satisfaction at having pleased her lord. The lady Bertha, although she saw the proud and tyrannical disposition of the baron, yet was so unsuspicious, and unconscious of any wicked views agitating in his mind, that she considered her own happiness as fixed and permanent, as far as respected his conduct towards her.

Every thing was now at peace at the castle. The witch was almost forgotten, or served only as a gossip's tale, for the domestics' fire-side in the hall. The mind of the baron was, however, ill at ease; at times his conscience raised apprehensions and horrors, which disturbed his repose in the midst of that indulgence, and security for wealth and grandeur, which his cruel immolation of the infant Edward had procured. The sight of the injured lady Bertha was often painful to him, and called him to an artful reconciliation with himself, grounded on the consequence that the other child Hugo would inherit the demesnes after his demise. This compromise lulled, at times, his conscience to sleep, and he began to think that there might be hopes even of pardon for him in another world.

The baron de La Braunch, having succeeded in removing the innocent object of his fear and aversion, had idly and falsely thought, that he should enjoy a course of uninterrupted days; he was astonished, therefore, to find that it could not be so: for at times the recollection of the means he had taken, for the security of his wealth, came across his mind, in a way that made him uneasy.

In addition to the restless sting of remorse, the baron felt another sensation disturb his mind: he began privately to dislike the lady Bertha; she sometimes, accidentally and unintentionally, reminded him of the mysterious loss of her little infant Edward; he was angry, too, that the child had not died of some disorder of nature, that he might have been spared the reflection of having been the instrument of its destruction.

Eleven years passed away in a sameness of occurrence at the castle, which, in a good family, would have constituted one of the most striking features of its domestic peace.

Old Doric frequently descanted on the strange and mysterious event of the infant Edward's loss, and endeavoured to account for it in various different ways; sometimes he insisted that the child was taken away to heaven; sometimes, that it was still alive, and had been ravished from the castle by some of the house of lord Edward of Martindale, who would rear it in obscurity, without a knowledge of its parents; so far, however, is the imputation of guilt from the great and powerful, that not the slightest suspicion fell on the baron.

During this time, the child Hugo grew up with all the fierce dispositions of his father, who caressed him chiefly on that account: he was bold, mischievous, ill-tempered, and obstinate. The servants of the castle, who all of them, at times, suffered from the propensity he had to tell tales and lies, began to have an aversion for him; not even the mild and tender manner of his lady mother could alter his perverse dispositions. The baron would not allow, on any occasion, that he should be thwarted, and his will was never to be contradicted by the domestics. The little Hugo was very cruel in his treatment of the poor animals who were about the castle; many of which were tortured for his amusement. He was, besides, so excessively indolent, that he would not be at the pains to learn any thing of the masters, who were engaged to teach him the accomplishments usually expected to be found in the young nobles destined for the court of Edward.

Old Doric had taken a dislike to his young master Hugo, because he laughed at the mathematics; but Jonas entertained some respect for him, as he was never backwards in drinking large quantities of sack and Burgundy, whenever offered him, which Jonas took as a good sign, and as a promise of his becoming a great man.

The lady Bertha endeavoured all she could, to correct the unseemly habits and dispositions of the child, but in vain; he grew up in the proud and sullen disposition of his father, and promised to be like him in every fault; an event, however, took place, which prevented the mischief such a temper might have done in the world. The child Hugo fell sick, and which was occasioned by a wilful exertion which he chose to make in the noon-day heat; not all the maternal care of the lady Bertha, nor all the skill of the first physicians of the king, could avail to check the raging fever that ensued, which baffled every endeavour, and triumphed over life; a circumstance which unfairly lessened the claims of the lady Bertha to the esteem and affection of her husband.

CHAPTER XXII

The palace of the lady Alwena.

WITHIN a few miles of the castle of La Braunch, near the brow of a high mountain fringed with underwood, stood the gorgeous palace of Alwena, which was known from afar by the height and beauty of its turrets, which were of the purest white, and of the most perfect architecture.

The palace of Alwena was the seat of pleasure. The way to it was through lanes of rose trees, by the side of a serpentine brook, which was one of the branches of the proud swelling Eden: whose banks bear the maiden primrose, the sweet-scented violet, the white lily, and the narcissus.

The front of the palace of Alwena was adorned with a hundred pillars of Parian marble, with pedestals and bases of red Corinthian stone, and entablatures of the most finished and exquisite workmanship. The porticos were double, with a two-fold range of columns; the gates were of ebony, and the balconies, from the windows of the palace, of the purest white ivory, as were also the galleries within this tasteful temple, the flooring of which was of the highest wrought mosaic. The walls were covered with the richest tapestry, and the furniture was the most elegant and superb.

The lady Alwena was a Dane by birth, but her education had been finished in the courts of Italy and France, and her manners partook largely of the licentiousness of those countries.

The lady Alwena was of uncommon stature; she was six feet four inches in height, and formed with an exquisite proportion, her limbs were in perfect symmetry, and she trod the ground with the grace and dignity of a princess; her countenance was as open and beautiful as the rich and luxuriant face of autumn; her eyes resembled sparkling gems; her cheeks were as the lily flower, tinged with the red rose; her lips were of a rich crimson, and her fine turned neck and bosom, were finished with the most exquisite workmanship of the hand of Nature, and outvied, in colour, the whiteness of the breast of the swan: her whole form was luxuriant, and teemed with the full ripeness of womanhood.

The lady Alwena had constantly refused every offer of marriage, since the death of her husband, lord Robert; which perhaps had been owing to her desire of reigning uncontrouled mistress of her indulgences and caprice.

Many reports, not at all favourable to the chastity of this lady, had been circulated during the life-time of her lord, while absent in the Holy-land; but since his death she had given loose to the reins of her passions, and had indulged herself in indiscriminate amours with several knights, who had become enamoured with her person; and who were discarded, as soon as her voluptuous appetites for variety had been gratified.

The lady Alwena was not only abandoned to the lust of unchaste desires, but her mind also was impure and wicked. She was proud, lofty, arrogant, overbearing, and revengeful; she could smile, and with the fascinating looks of love, but her heart was full of hatred, and bitter reproach of virtue; her mind was prostituted and debased; she was ever busy, and seeking to demolish the fair structure of female chastity, wherever she found it erected, and was constantly active in spreading calumnies that might destroy the good fame and reputation of the virtuous ladies of the court.

The lady Alwena, who had only just taken possession of her splendid palace, was soon made acquainted with the baron's close neighbourhood to her, and with the character of the amiable lady Bertha; she had long known that of the baron de La Braunch, his high rank, and achievements.

CHAPTER XXIII

The Baron's interview with the Lady Alwena.

THE lady Alwena desired to become acquainted with the baron de La Braunch, both from her wicked propensity to disturb, if possible, the happiness of the good lady Bertha, and from her inclination to enlist the baron in her train of admirers; and she had already formed in her mind the cruel project of rivalling the lady Bertha in the esteem and affections of her lord.

Occasion and opportunity is not long wanting to the wicked; lady Alwena frequented the hunt, where she distinguished herself by her astonishing intrepidity, and skill in riding, which was unequalled.

One day the baron happened to fall in with the chase at which she was present, and beheld her perform astonishing feats of horsemanship, in the pursuit of a gaunt wolf. The baron became enamoured with her figure and beauty, and approached her with all the gallantry of a courteous and well-bred knight. The lady Alwena was not wanting, on her side, in that finished courtesy which is displayed by the ladies of the court.

The baron, after the chase was over, offered to conduct the lady Alwena to her castle, and the offer, in the presence of several other knights, was most graciously accepted.

On her arrival at the palace, the lady Alwena retired to her apartment to dress, and left the baron to visit the gardens, accompanied by her esquire.

Every thing that could charm and delight the senses, was collected in the apartments and gardens of the palace of Alwena; birds of the most beautiful plumage were displayed, and the sweetest sounds of the different songsters of the grove were heard, as well as of music, concealed from the sight, but which resembled, in harmony, the lyre, and the harp.

The orange and jessamine formed lanes through the entrances, and spread a gentle and odoriferous atmosphere; soft music was made to play in the avenues, as if by magic, and fountains of transparent fluid played wantonly in these apartments of pleasure, where the richly decorated couch gave invitation to repose, or voluptuousness.

The luxuries of taste, and splendour, were well suited to delight the disturbed and restless mind of the baron, which was never satisfied, unless pampered with some new invention, or gratification; his depraved appetite required to be excited with something beyond the refreshment sought after by pure and elegant minds.

The lady Alwena descended from her apartment, attired in the most bewitching manner; her woman, Constante, versed in all the arts and mysteries of attraction, had so disposed the drapery of her dress, that her elegant form was seen through the fine texture of her linen; her bosom, which was rich in the luxuriancies of nature, was enough uncovered to show the perfection of its form; her head was adorned with the richest jewels, in the form of a star, composed of the chrysolite, the green emerald, the sapphire, and the onyx, and her arms were adorned with rich bracelets of diamonds.

The baron, who was naturally of an amorous complexion, was astonished at the display of so many charms; his imagination teemed with such rapturous images of the beauties of the lady Alwena's person, that he dwelt upon it in amazement, and immediately longed for the possession; he did not, however, know the price that he was to pay; he had to deal with a woman versed in intrigue, and who knew how to tantalize her admirers; her grand and majestic air supplied the place of modesty, for her protection, and forbad the too near approach of her admirers; and after some conversation, and taking refreshment of the most exquisite fruits and wines, the baron returned to the castle, fired with a fatal passion that nothing could extinguish.

The baron had now fresh engagements and occupations to fill up his time; he forsook his accustomed habits, and his former pursuits were neglected; he used no more the exercises of the chase, unless the lady Alwena was present, and the achievements of the tournament were surrendered to the study of the decorations of his person, the splendour of his equipage, and his attendants; he made daily visits to the palace of Alwena, and, delighted with the enchanting beauty of its owner, and with her fascinating conversation, began already to neglect his usual attentions to the lady Bertha, who began to notice the alteration of the behaviour, and the increasing coldness and indifference of her lord, but was too unsuspicious, and good, to attribute it to the dishonourable cause.

The circumstance of the death of the infant Hugo, which the baron would at any time before have mourned as the most cruel of events, lost all its bitterness, in the contemplation of the delightful solace that he could now find in the company of the lady Alwena.

Lady Alwena was well informed of the extensive demesnes of the baron, and of the principalities he enjoyed in the right of his wife, and which had now absolutely become his own, by the death of the infant Edward; she knew, too, that his ambition was never at rest, and began to feel that, were it not for the family of lady Bertha, he would gladly forsake her, the first opportunity that offered; nor was she wrong in her conjectures, for the baron had already begun to contemplate the possibility of one day or other getting rid of her. The affair, however, was difficult: some of her illustrious relatives were alive in the Holy-land, and he feared that in case he should use her ill, his conduct would be one day severely called in question.

The artful Alwena had, by degrees, acquired an entire ascendancy over the mind and actions of the baron. She had forsaken the reserve and delicacy proper to her sex, and had, by her endearments and caresses, as by magic, overpowered the functions of his mind.

The baron was so great a slave to his passion, that he was determined to make every obstacle yield to its indulgence, and to the attainment of the object. The lady Bertha, full of health, and as serene in mind as the good, in sorrow, always are, promised no early termination of her relationship with the baron. The Hag, therefore, occurred to his mind, as the proper person to consult on the occasion; he knew that she had the most horrid aversion to that estimable woman, and that she would gladly assist in the accomplishment of his ends, and which seemed to promise the fulfilment of her own prediction.

END OF THE FIRST VOLUME.

The Witch of Ravensworth

Volume II

CHAPTER I

The Baron renews his Visits to the Hag.

MANY years had elapsed, since the baron had taken any notice of the Hag: he had obtained his object, through her diabolical machinations, and, having had no further occasion for her services, had forgot his agent; the witch, however, now came to his recollection, as the best person he could consult, in his present difficulty.

The baron, therefore, resolved to pay a visit to his old acquaintance, and to engage her, by means of new promises, in his service.

It was one evening, as soon as the sun had sunk beneath the horizon, that the baron set out, alone, to visit the wretch, on whose wickedness he hoped to depend for success.

The baron found the Hag, as usual, seated on her joint-stool, mumbling her incantations by the fire-side.

The witch affected not to know the baron: she inquired who he was, and why he disturbed her?

"I am," cried he, "thy friend, the baron de La Braunch."

"Oh, oh!" answered the witch; "how kind, to call and see the poor old woman, and how grateful too, to come so soon! I dare say, now, that it is from pure affection that thou hast come. Thou dost not want my assistance! no, no; it would be wronging the noble nature of the baron de La Braunch, to think so!"

Nothing could be more malicious than the looks of the witch, as she spoke these words, and uttered her reproaches.

It was some time before the baron could appease the Hag, sufficiently to explain the state of his mind; which task he had no sooner performed, than she raised herself up. "Oh, oh!" cried the witch; "there is business to be done, and therefore thou art come. Truly now I suppose that thou dost think, that the powers whom I serve have nothing to do, but to wish for the accomplishment of thy wishes; but the matter is not so easy as thou mayst think: Askar the fiend, my master, must be courted to this; thou must see the demon thyself."

The baron started.

"Yes, thou must see him in all his horrors; thou must visit the illuminated castle, and at midnight thou must become the associate of devils. Why, did not the baron promise that he would come to our feast? how well he kept his word!"

57

"Ha!" cried the baron, "what dost thou ask? why must I visit those infernal orgies? is not thy power sufficient to obtain my wishes? it is thy agency alone I want; nor will I have any other."

"Then," cried the Hag, "I cannot do thee service."

"How! dost thou refuse me then?"

"I have not the power, baron, to aid thy wishes."

"Not the power!"

"No," returned the Hag; "my dominion is over infants, innocent infants."

The baron started.

"My power is over the plants, the herbage, and the cattle and flocks of the field; but to oppress or destroy the suffering virtuous, in man or woman, is a strong work, and needs the aid of the greater spirits: but despair not, baron; shew thyself fearless, and fond of blood, and the mighty Askar will shew thee means of success; he will give thee his power, his protection."

"I will serve thy master, then," cried the baron.

"Charming!" replied the witch.

"Tell me," cried the baron, "when shall I witness these horrid mysteries?"

"This day se'nnight," returned the witch, "is one of our grand meetings. Thou must not visit us before darkness shall have added its glooms to the face of the black heath, nor until the screech-owl shall have begun to hoot; then visit the Hag, and she will lead thee to the enjoyment of delightful horrors, and games and gambols of devils, where thou shalt see them sup, and sup with them too: be punctual; thou knowest my desire to serve thee!"

The baron took his leave of the witch, big with apprehensions of the events which were to follow, ill pleased with the injunction of the witch, and yet well pleased at the prospect it presented, of obtaining the full gratification of his wishes.

CHAPTER II

The Baron changes his Behaviour to the lady Bertha.

THE baron had no sooner begun to entertain hopes of the accomplishment of his desires, and to find himself at liberty to act towards his lady as he pleased, than he began to show her indifference, and the most mortifying neglect; he wished, indeed, to wean her from him; and though it was no easy task, from her natural goodness of heart, for her to understand so cruel an experiment, yet she began to fear that, with the death of her child, she had lost the affections of her lord. This idea preyed upon her mind, and her melancholy the artful baron took occasion to interpret as ill temper; an accusation as unjust, as it was ungenerous.

The lady Bertha little knew, however, the dangers which awaited her, or the wicked connexion the baron had formed with the abandoned Alwena.

This conduct of the baron relieved him considerably from the task of duplicity; yet not entirely, as he was aware that he must preserve some appearance of respect and attention for his lady, as, otherwise the completion of his plans might create suspicion among his vassals.

CHAPTER III

The Baron is presented, by the Hag, to the Fiend.

THE night had arrived for the baron's visit to the witch.

An utter darkness was spread over the scenery of the heath. It promised to be a night of horrors.

The baron stepped forward, as unwilling to encounter new objects of terror. Scarcely could he discern the path. At every instant he heard voices of distress; he saw, too, lights at a distance, which presently vanished, and were seen no more. The owl hooted, the ravens croaked, as disturbed from their roosts, and airy substances flitted across his path. Not a human creature was to be seen.

At length the baron arrived at the door of the Hag's dwelling.

He lifted up the latch; the witch was not there.

He surveyed the room.

The large grey cat walked round him three times, and snuffed the air.

The Hag entered; her lamp was in her hand.

She desired the baron to follow her.

She enjoined him not to utter a syllable.

The glimmering of the lamp discovered only a long, vaulted, passage, closely covered.

Presently they came to an open space.

The witch threw a mantle over the face of the baron.

They proceeded.

The baron heard strange sounds, like loud music; a chorus of singing voices, mingled with groans and shrieks.

In an instant the witch withdrew the mantle from before the face of the baron.

A sudden light appeared.

His eyes were dazzled with innumerable burning tapers.

For an instant, he could discern no other object.

Presently his eyes were stunned with a horrid laugh, and yell.

It was the nocturnal inhabitants performing their midnight mysteries and revels.

The baron, accompanied by the Hag, ascended a flight of broad steps, into a spacious apartment, from whence the noise of the voices was heard.

The Hag stooped to the floor, from whence she took two large, sounding, brass cymbals, laid at the entrance. These she struck forcibly together, uttering the words "Calama, calama."

Immediately a horrid scream and laugh was heard, from the inner part of the saloon, which was instantly succeeded by a perfect stillness.

The baron now first discovered a throne, covered with black, on which was sitting a figure, the face of which was pale, and smeared with blood. It was fantastically drest, in a party-coloured habit, red and black. It had a silver crown upon its head. The head and arms of a skeleton lay at its feet; and before the throne stood a small altar of granate, on which was placed a bowl, filled with a liquid that resembled human blood.

Presently, six fantastic figures appeared. They were drest in black, and had girdles around them, of a red colour. Each one of them had a tinkling bell in their hand, which they rung violently as they danced, and practised various gambols.

The six figures led in with them a milk-white lamb, dressed with ribands and flowers, which they tied, by one of its feet, to the altar, and which they had no sooner performed, than they ran furiously round the saloon, with the most frantic gestures.

In the midst of the hall was a pure flame, burning in a large censer.

The six figures arranged themselves, three on each side of the fiend who was seated on the throne.

The Hag approached before the baron. She knelt at the foot of the throne. She repeated the words, "*Calama, calama;*" at which the devils shouted a cry of joy.

The baron stood dismayed.

The witch beckoned to him to approach. She whispered him, "Fie, fie; be assured, noble baron!"

He was offended at the bare suggestion of his being afraid.

He frowned on the witch, and walked boldly forward.

His steps echoed as he trod through the hall.

The witch whispered again in his ear, "Attend, and silently observe our mysteries."

The fiend ordered the Hag to withdraw.

The baron was left among the demons.

"Thou wouldst enjoy," cried the fiend, "wealth and beauty both; thou wouldst have honour, and pamper thyself with the richest treats of voluptuous nature, thou wouldst have all that Mammon and Lucifer can bestow, and thou shalt have them; but thou must first prove thyself worthy of these gifts: thou must be initiated in our mysteries."

The baron bowed his head.

"Approach," cried the fiend, "to the altar."

The baron approached the altar.

He was directed to draw the dagger from his side; he was desired to dip its point in the bowl of blood; he was to pronounce the words "Calama, calama."

The fiend who was on the throne desired the baron to look stedfastly on the western entrance.

The baron was undismayed. He looked stedfastly on the door. He beheld a female form enter. It was the same that he had seen at his second visit to the Hag; but it approached nearer. It held a cup in one hand; it waved the other to the baron.

The baron was appalled; a cold perspiration ran down his limbs; the spectre glided away; all was still; the baron remained in suspense.

Presently the blast of a trumpet was heard.

The Hag entered at the sound.

She dragged at her heels a loathsome carcase.

It was the same female form that had just appeared.

It was no longer a spirit; it was a body, but without life.

The baron shuddered.

"It is now," cried the Hag, "that thou must prove thyself worthy of the friendship of the mighty Askar, the prince of mischief, of disease, of death, and of horror. Now thou must prove thy soul undaunted; and then thou mayst go and sleep securely in the bed of the beautiful Alwena.

"What is it more," cried the baron, "that thou wouldst I should perform to please thee?"

"I prepare to tell thee," cried the witch, with looks of frightful exultation. "Thou must plunge thy dagger, embrued as it is with blood, in the bosom of this body."

"Of that body?" cried the baron, viewing it with horror.

"Obey," cried the Hag; "thy hopes depend on thy obedience: 'tis the will of Askar."

The baron looked again on the form of the female at his feet; he trembled; he looked in its face; he turned from it with aversion; he lifted up the dagger; he hesitated; his nervous arm trembled.

"Strike!" cried the Hag.

The baron made an effort; he turned his face, and plunged the dagger in the breast of the corpse.

In an instant a horrid and incessant yell was heard.

The pure flame, which was burning in the censer, became a thick, black, smoke.

A malignant vapour filled the saloon.

The fiend on the throne handed the baron a scroll, on which was written— *"The Promise of Askar to the Baron de La Braunch:— the Death of Lady Bertha, and the Possession of Alwena."*

The scroll was instantly closed.

The Hag was told to withdraw.

The baron withdrew with the Hag.

They pursued the same passage; they arrived at the hovel.

"Well, baron," cried the witch, "thine is a noble career; thou art in high favour; all will be as thou couldst wish, to-morrow night. To-morrow night, at twelve, leave the subterraneous passage to the castle free, that the Hag may enter without being seen. Give me but admittance to the chamber of lady Bertha; then leave me to my work: but no mortal being must be nigh; the Hag must be undisturbed. I have a knife and will do the business speedily. Her body must be given an offering to the fiend. Then thou shalt see it breathless; and, when the revolving months shall have produced a year, from this time, then thou wilt have a festival to keep; thou wilt have the same duty to perform, that thou hast done this night."

"Why is it," cried the baron, "that I must be tormented with these horrors?"

"Because," replied the Hag, "IT IS THE PRICE OF PLEASURE. Thou wouldst have riches, and the charms of woman, and honours, and enjoyment."

"Enjoyment!" repeated the baron.

"Yes," cried the Hag; "ere the convent bell shall have rung to vespers, to-morrow evening, thou shalt be freed from all the obstacles that prevent thy happiness."

"'Tis well," cried the baron; "then this night rids me of my restraints."

"Thou wilt be free to dalliance, Askar has promised it."

CHAPTER IV

The Fate of Lady Bertha.

THE baron, with his excellent duplicity, on the next morning, appeared to his lady unusually gay and cheerful. He inquired kindly how she had slept; and was so courteous, that her heart was rejoiced, in the hope that the baron had renewed his affections towards her: her innocent mind little suspected the danger that awaited her at night.

At length the hour arrived.

The baron waited, in anxious expectation, for the witch.

The baron had ordered the attendants of lady Bertha to withdraw; she did not want them.

The baron, himself, pleaded an excuse for leaving her; he had letters to write.

The convent bell had rung.

The baron retired to his study, where he remained an hour, in hopes that the business was going on.

At length, he descended a few steps; he heard a groan.

He proceeded no further.

He listened: all was still.

He stepped gently down.

The word "Calama" was written against the wall; it was the sign that the work was completed.

The baron, with that composure, and daring effrontery, which he possessed in so eminent a degree, instantly called one of the female attendants, and desired her to seek the lady Bertha; he wished to sup with her, in her apartment.

The attendant went on this errand; but could not find her lady, in any part of the castle.

She called Ranetrude.

Ranetrude had not seen her for more than an hour. She went in search of her; but in vain. She trembled at some conclusions which rushed on her mind; she was shocked at this new circumstance of terror.

The attendant was afraid to return to the baron with the tidings.

At length he called Ranetrude by name.

She obeyed the summons, and informed the baron, that her search after her lady had been fruitless.

The baron affected a surprise and anger, that made the domestics tremble for the consequences.

The lady Bertha had never left the castle, to go abroad, without her attendants.

There was no circumstance, within the reach of probability, unthought of, or unattended to.

The baron dispatched his attendants different ways, in search of the lady Bertha.

He went, himself, to every avenue of the castle, and through the extensive galleries.

Hathbrand suggested, that perhaps the Hag had had some hand in this new catastrophe.

The baron listened with attention.

"Truly," cried he, with perfect coolness, "we have, as you know, before, accused the witch, when the little Edward had disappeared from among us; yet we were not able to substantiate any charge against her; we had no proof of her guilt."

The baron kept Hathbrand a considerable time in conversation, on the subject of what was best to be done.

There were hopes, that she had walked to enjoy the refreshing air; she might have chosen to be alone; she might have wished to be free from restraint; she was fond of contemplation.

The evening arrived; lady Bertha had not returned: the darkness of night came on; lady Bertha had not arrived.

The draw-bridges were not raised as usual.

A fresh guard were mounted on the battlements.

Orders were given to admit any strangers who might bring intelligence.

The next morning arrived, and brought no news of lady Bertha.

A week elapsed; lady Bertha was not found.

At length, the baron sent for the obsequious Hathbrand.

He represented the propriety of spreading a report, without the walls of the castle, that lady Bertha had died suddenly: he considered it the best way to prevent the inquiries of idle curiosity.

The submissive Hathbrand acquiesced.

By the instructions of the baron, he acquainted the other domestics, that the body of lady Bertha was found. She had wandered from the castle, near the river; by accident, she had fallen into the stream; she was drowned, and had been taken to the convent.

The baron confined himself, for some days, to the castle.

The domestics were given mourning.

A burial of one of the sisters of the convent was said to be lady Bertha's; the report gained ground: the gratifications of curiosity are soon satisfied; it swallows a bait without difficulty, and is pleased with any thing like news.

CHAPTER V

*The Baron visits the Palace of Askar; views the
Corpse of Lady Bertha*

THE baron had now a task to perform: he had to make his promised visit to the fiend; a duty which, depraved as he was, he could not think of without disgust.

The night arrived; he found the Hag ready to receive him, and to conduct him to the chamber of horrors.

The witch led the baron, covered with his mantle, in the way she had before done, to the palace of Askar.

It was empty of its dreadful inhabitants.

There was not any thing to be seen, but the altar, and throne, with a bier, placed in the middle of the room. On the bier was laid the body of lady Bertha.

The Hag led the baron to the altar.

She required from him an horrid injunction; his hair stood on end, as she pronounced the sentence: he was to plunge his dagger in the bosom.

The baron shuddered, and obeyed.

"Behold, now," cried the witch, "the reward of all thy hardi-hood, and labour; thy fears and difficulties are at an end: thou mayst visit the lovely Alwena, and pass the hours in voluptuous dalliance. Thou art arrived to that desired point, when every thing is accomplished. Away, then, and enjoy! Even now the lady Alwena expects thee; she smiles, and courts thee to her bed. Thou knowest not the delights which await thee: but, first, take a farewell salute of thy sweet lady here."

"Accursed Hag!" cried the baron, "hold thy tongue; all is abomination here; torment me no further."

"Nay, now, this childishness will offend the mighty Askar. Do not be ungrateful, baron. Come, come, I see that thou art not yet a man."

The Hag now conducted the baron to her hovel.

He seated himself on the chair; he leaned against the wall.

Not even the lascivious images he had painted to his mind, of the possession of such charms as lady Alwena's, could prevent the horrors of reproach, and disgust, which the dreadful injunction he had obeyed brought to his recollection.

The Hag observed these changes in the mind of the baron.

"Come," cried she, "thou hast no more ill acts to perform; thou needst not let thy conscience perplex thee thus; away, and be merry."

The baron took his leave of the Hag, and, after arriving at the castle, drest to pay a visit to the lady Alwena; it was the first time that he had seen her, since the death of lady Bertha.

She received him with her usual complacency and dignity; but, seeing him out of spirits, made use of those soft, winning airs, which an artful woman knows too well how to practise: she leaned towards him; she pressed her bosom against him; she invited him, as it were, to soothe the anguish of a disturbed mind, in that luxu-rious mansion of loveliness and beauty.

The baron, as she reclined towards him, viewed the perfect excellence of her form; he was fired with passion, and, in the ea-gerness of desire, laid his riches and honours at her feet.

The ambitious Alwena, who not any knight would have cho-sen to wed, felt a secret triumph: she, however, managed artfully to govern her feelings; she affected a reserve and dignity; she desired a week to consider of his proposal; but, at the same time, she tempered her reserve with such wanton and bewitching glances, as gave him no reason to doubt his success.

The lady Alwena gave the baron her hand, at parting, with a promise, not to keep him longer in suspense, than the time she had fixed.

The baron retired to the castle, with his mind filled with the most delightful images of his approaching happiness, and, so sensual and depraved was his imagination, that he thought of nothing but the possession of her person, and passed away the whole of his time in the contemplation of her charms.

At length the week expired, and the baron was punctual, to obtain the answer of the haughty Alwena.

He waited on her himself. She received him, however, in a way that gave him no reason to hope for success: her countenance was lofty and stern; she smiled, 'tis true; but it appeared the smile of scorn.

The baron was assiduous, and abject.

An opportunity offered: her attendants had retired. The baron entreated her to pronounce his sentence.

The lady Alwena, with an air of arrogance, placed a scroll of parchment in his hands.

The baron received it with a low bow; he unfurled the scroll.

On the scroll were written the words—"*The Lady Alwena consents to become the Bride of the Baron de La Braunch.*"

CHAPTER VI

The Marriage of Lady Alwena and the Baron.

THE day of the nuptials arrived, and the sun shone forth in its full radiance, as it were, to add its brilliancy to the occasion.

The domestics were occupied in the like preparations, as for the marriage of lady Bertha; they were not, however, so happy, and satisfied, on the occasion: they regretted the mysterious death of their dear lady. Old Doric could not reconcile that event; he wanted demonstration of the fact of her being drowned by accident; he had his suspicions, but dared not even to hint. Jonas was versed in no science, but the doctrine of fluids, and in that he had dipt pretty deeply. It was all the same to Jonas who was mistress, so that he kept the place of butler.

The marriage ceremony was to be performed at the palace of Alwena.

A tournament was to be had on the occasion.

Numerous of the domestics, and tenantry, were seen busily employed, in placing spears and shields at each end of the ground, for the tilters.

A superb stand, hung with crimson, and decorated with streamers and banners, was erected for the lady Alwena.

Under the stand hung, by chains, two massy shields, one silver, and the other red.

The ceremony of the marriage took place at the chapel of the palace.

The bride was drest in white silk raiment, ornamented with gold-work. She wore, over her dress, a mantle of crimson.

The baron was in armour, and bore, on his head, the helmet which he had taken from a Saracen, at Palestine.

The holy rites were performed by father Velaschi.

No Hag appeared, to interrupt the ceremony.

The company invited were the most distinguished barons and knights, within twenty miles round.

The marriage ceremony having been concluded, the company took their seats in the stands, to see the tournament.

CHAPTER VII

The Tournament.

THE tilts were now about to commence.

The trumpets sounded from each side, and the heralds took their respective stations.

The baron, and the lady Alwena, entered their gallery, and all the people present were astonished at the beauty, and sumptuous apparel, of the bride.

The constable of the castle, Hathbrand, descended the steps, and, after making his obeisance to the crowd, placed himself on the chair of state, at the foot of the steps of the gallery, where was the throne.

Six knights appeared, on each side, attended by their pages, who began, already, to gird on their masters' swords.

The knights ranged themselves in order, their spears placed upright on their thighs, and their pages standing at their horses' heads, holding the bridles.

The knights, previous to engaging, made, each of them, an obeisance, first to the lady Alwena, then to the baron, and then to the ladies who were in the gallery, spectators of the tournay; which salutation was returned, by the ladies waving their handkerchiefs.

A knight of considerable prowess, in black armour, with a red plume in his helmet, now stepped forward, and, with the point of his spear, touched the silver shield, in token of challenge to the tournay, and then returned to his place.

A knight from the opposite side, performed the same ceremony.

Presently the lists became full.

The constable then rose, and, turning himself to the lady Alwena, made a low obeisance, which she returned, with the most gracious condescension, and courtesy.

The constable then waved his right hand, as a signal to the trumpets.

A young knight now came forward. He was drest in white armour, which shone like silver; his helmet was blue, adorned with a green feather. He opposed himself to the knight of the black armour.

Every one felt solicitous for the success of the brave and gallant youth, thus unequally matched. They knew the prowess, and gigantic strength, of the knight of the black armour, and trembled for the fate of the young knight.

The eyes of the lady Alwena were fixed, the whole time, on the knight of the white armour. The gracefulness of his form, the elegance of his manners, and his gallant appearance, had, already, attracted her attention; already she admired, and loved him; nor could she disguise her sentiments: those who knew lady Alwena, discovered, by her looks, the state of her mind; the baron de La Braunch was, alone, ignorant of the regards she paid the stranger; he could not have imagined such depravity on the day of her marriage.

The trumpets now sounded a charge, and two of the knights engaged desperately; one of them was unhorsed.

Two others now entered the lists; and one of them shared the like fate.

Again the trumpets gave a flourish; which was the summons for the young knight, in the white armour, to come to tournay.

He advances, on his milk-white courser.

The knight in the black armour awaits him.

They engage.

The knight in the black armour seems as he would fall like a thunderbolt on the youthful knight. The young knight is, however, dexterous and agile in arms.

The knight of the black armour is dismounted; and shouts and acclamations of joy rend the sky.

They retire for a time.

The tournay on foot begins, and other knights engage.

Presently, the knights in the black and white armour are refreshed. They engage anew. They engage with their swords; their falchions strike fire; and they contend for the victory, foot to foot, and hand to hand. At length, the knight in the black armour is beaten to the ground. He fights for some time; he is overpowered.

Now the combatants, once more, mount their steeds; the trumpet sounds again; and the three knights together, engage the other three. Again the knight in the white armour is successful: he is declared conqueror.

The lady Alwena presents him, with her own hand, the rich sword, the prize of the tournay. He receives it with the most graceful address.

The constable of the tournay demands his title. He is called Alaric, the Knight of the White Armour. The name of Alaric resounds through the ranks of the spectators.

The lady Alwena now rises from her seat; the justs end. She honours the youthful knight, Alaric, with the most distinguishing glances of approbation: he returns them, with a courtesy and expression, and with such polished manners, as astonish even the lady Alwena, educated, as she had been, in foreign courts; but Alaric was of the court of France, where were the flower of chivalry.

The young Alaric became the talk, the admiration, of all the ladies present at the tournament; but his gallantry had made a more considerable progress in the heart of lady Alwena.

The lady Alwena, forgetful of the delicacy and chastity of her sex, was enamoured with the young knight, and honoured him with such distinguishing glances of preference, as would have made any man of gallantry vain; nor were they lost on the accomplished chevalier of the court of France.

CHAPTER VIII

The Ball.

THE first day of the next week was fixed for the splendid ball, to be given by the baron de La Braunch, on the occasion of his marriage with the lady Alwena.

The palace of Alwena was the scene of all these sumptuous preparations.

At length the evening arrives. The grand saloon already begins to fill. The illuminated porticos, the wax-tapers, ranged in order, through the entrances, the burning censers, filled with frankincense, all presented an air of magic, and fascination, that engaged the mind to pleasure.

The tables were spread with the most exquisite viands, served to the guests by little boys, naked, but furnished with wings, and with bows, and quivers full of arrows; others, as young Bacchanals, presented, in golden cups, the richest Rhenish and Burgundy.

Each knight led his lady into the saloon, drest in the most elegant fashion. Each lady had her hair bound, and ornamented with a fillet, studded with precious stones. Their drapery was of the finest silk, or linens; and their bosoms exposed, as far as modest taste would permit. They bore, on their dresses, the escutcheons of their different lords, and bracelets of pearl, and jewels of many sorts, decorated their hands and feet.

The lady Alwena was seated near the baron de La Braunch, on a throne, to receive her guests. She was, when standing, the finest figure in the room, and considerably taller than any of the other ladies: her face was a perfect oval; her eyes blue, and filled with a fascinating sweetness and voluptuousness, not unmixed, however, with the sparkling glances of pride, and scorn; her elegant arched eyebrows gave a grandeur to her countenance; and her forehead seemed properly destined to bear a diadem; her nose was of the Grecian model; her cheeks soft, and of a transparent bloom; her mouth of the colour of the ruby; and her teeth of the purest white enamel.

From the face, downward, it was impossible to view the perfect form of Alwena with Platonic regard. Her neck was united, insensibly, to her shoulders; and her alabaster bosom, swelling with every movement, displayed the richest treasures of voluptuous nature; her arms were of the most exquisite form, and her limbs so perfectly in symmetry, that her majestic height gave no uneasiness to her action, which was as graceful as could be imagined.

The only knight who was without a lady, was the young Alaric; but Alwena sufficiently made up this deficiency to him, by the most particular attentions.

The ball had now begun, and Alaric led the beautiful Alwena to the dance.

The baron sought the honour of another lady's hand.

All was gaiety and pleasure. The music played the most enchanting measures; and the feet of the dancers moved to the sprightly sounds of love and rapture.

On a sudden the dancers stopt; an alarm was given: a foul figure presented itself among the company.

It stood on the left of lady Alwena; it took her hand; it whispered her.

It was the Hag.

The baron stood aghast; he did not dare to interfere.

At length lady Alwena spoke:—"Poor old woman!" said she; "she comes with courtesy and good wishes towards us. It is the celebration of our nuptials: she comes to wish us joy."

The baron bowed.

With an air of dignity, lady Alwena ordered her attendants to show the Hag to an apartment, and that she should be served with the most exquisite dainties, and with the most delicious of the wines.

The Hag retired, without uttering a syllable.

She looked in the face of the baron, as she withdrew; she smiled; a convulsive laugh was on her face.

The baron could not help being confounded at the behaviour of lady Alwena to the witch: he knew her to be more proud and arrogant than himself; he could not reconcile the complacency of her conduct to the Hag.—"Surely," cried the baron, "the lady Alwena is not acquainted with the Hag!"

The baron took an opportunity to ask his lady, in a careless and indifferent manner, if she had ever seen that troublesome old woman before?

The lady Alwena replied, without the least hesitation—"Never."

The mind of the baron de La Braunch was relieved; he was happy that the affair had ended in the way it had.

The doors of the saloon were now thrown open.

The tables in the supper-rooms were prepared.

The ladies, attended by their knights, took their places. Alaric was placed, by Alwena, next herself.

The board was spread with the most delicious meats and fruits; and the wines were contained in the richest golden vases of Roman model.

The most enchanting sounds, that the skill of the minstrels could produce, were heard, during supper; many healths were drunk, and all the company seemed delighted with the entertainment afforded them by the baron.

Lady Alwena presented her guests with the choicest delicacies, and amused them with the most witty and enchanting conversation. Every eye was engaged in contemplating her beauty, and every ear occupied in listening to her discourse.

Presently her bright eyes began to sparkle, with the intoxicating draughts she had taken, of wine and pleasure.

Her looks were now no longer directed to the baron; her attentions were paid elsewhere; her eyes were now soft and languishing, when she fixed them on Alaric; they view the baron de La Braunch with scorn.

The lady Alwena was unguarded in the expressions she used to Alaric.

Presently, in the madness of wine and lust, she took the red feather which was in the helmet of Alaric, that stood on the board, and placed it in her own hair.

The baron could no longer dissemble; he reddened with anger; he whispered to her: she disdained to answer.

The whole company observed the conduct of lady Alwena.

The young knight Alaric, himself, blushed at her behaviour, and was confounded.

The festivity of the scene was at an end; every one seemed to wish that they were away, and at length the party withdrew.

No sooner had the ladies, attended by their knights, withdrawn from the hall, than the baron gave the lady Alwena some glances of his disapprobation; his countenance lowered, and he did not deign to shew her the slightest attentions.

The lady Alwena smiled at the gloominess of his temper; she inquired, with a sarcastic sneer, if any thing had offended him?

He reminded her of her behaviour to the young Alaric.

"Truly!" returned the lady Alwena, "are my looks and actions to be examined with so much jealous scrutiny? am I to be watched?"

"There was no occasion for that," replied the baron: "all were witnesses of your particular attention."

The lady Alwena spurned at this reproach, and, in the best of her resentment, replied to the baron—"Knight, it is not for thee to controul the actions, much less the looks, of lady Alwena; her high pretensions must not yield to slavery; be satisfied, mighty sir, if, at times, she condescends to favour thee with those smiles she can bestow on her favourites: thou dost not know Alwena; but thou mightst have heard, that the most illustrious and gallant kneel at her feet, and court her to be kind."

"Yes," replied the baron, in a haughty tone; "the baron had heard, and knows enough, already, to make him think it prudent to forbid the approaches of the presumptuous Alaric."

"And is that thy design, most noble baron?" cried the lady Alwena; "truly, then, thou wilt find thyself mistaken."

"Lady," returned the baron, "I command, that thou shalt never see him more!"

"Indeed!" cried the lady Alwena.

"It is my will."

"Is it? then thus, baron, does the lady Alwena show her contempt for her new alliance:" with these words, she tore the escutcheon of her lord from the right shoulder of her robe; she trampled it under foot; it was with an air of sovereign contempt and defiance.

"Lady Alwena," cried the baron, "thou art mad! away to thy chamber."

The lady Alwena disdained to move.

At length the baron, with a stern look, quitted the chamber; he retired to his own room; he ruminated on the events of the day: he was uneasy, and disturbed in mind; he began to fear, that the lady Alwena's proud, imperious temper, would prove a torment to him: he had obtained possession of the charms he lusted after, and, though his appetite was not palled, he did not feel the like adoration which he had done.

The baron could not be said to retire to rest: his jealousy, his pride, were both alarmed; his hopes of future happiness were considerably damped; every thing conspired to disturb and vex him.

CHAPTER IX

The Misery of the Wicked.—A Reconciliation,
followed by another Quarrel

THE lady Alwena, on reflection, began, on her side, to think that she had gone too far: she did not wish for an absolute quarrel with the baron; but, such was her impetuous and ungovernable temper, that she found it difficult, and, at times, impossible, to curb: she had been used to an entire sovereignty over men; and her favourites, even, were her vassals; those who paid her the highest homage, and who flattered her most, in the presence of others were permitted.

The next morning, as both parties were inclined to peace, they met with a mutual complacency: they knew, that each of them were depraved and wretched beings; and they considered, that it was their mutual interest to agree: the baron, therefore, behaved as if nothing had happened; and lady Alwena, with consummate art, touched delicately on the cause of their quarrel: she hinted, that the baron, by his injurious suspicions, had excited a little desire of revenge in her breast, as, she said, it would in the breast of any woman; and, that her attentions to the young knight, Alaric, had been solely on that account.

The baron politely accepted this interpretation of his lady's conduct; and a reconciliation took place, attended with all those flattering expressions of regard, which are so frequently the language of insincerity.

The baron, whose mind was relieved considerably by this discourse, and who was flattered by the condescension, as he thought it, of the lady Alwena, promised himself a source of enjoyment in that alliance; he sought, therefore, to pay every attention to her inclinations, and, while he left her perfect mistress of her conduct, he amused himself, when absent from her, as he was formerly accustomed to do, at the hunt, or in the exercise of arms with his brother knights.

One day, having returned early from the chase, being unwell, the baron retired to his apartment, when he heard some music playing in the gallery, near the apartment of lady Alwena; which circumstance attracted his attention; he walked, therefore, along the gallery, and entered the room which adjoined hers, unnoticed by any one; which room was an anti-chamber, with a window that overlooked her apartment.

The baron heard that lady Alwena was in conversation with some one within, and, his pride and jealousy being awakened, he looked through the window of the anti-chamber, from whence he beheld the young knight, Alaric, in gentle dalliance with the lady Alwena.

The baron would, at first, have called the knight to account for this discovery; but he prudently checked his emotions of anger for the moment; he considered, that such a woman as lady Alwena would have her favourites, if lord Alaric was disposed of, and that to quarrel on her account, would be endless, if not fatal.

The baron waited, therefore, in his chamber, until the accustomed hour of his return, by which time, he knew the knight, Alaric, would be dismissed; it was then that he visited the chamber of lady Alwena, and accused her, bluntly, of having received a visit from the knight.

At first, the lady Alwena seemed disposed to contradict this assertion; but, being wise enough to think that that would not avail, she summoned arrogance sufficient to say—"Well, sir, what then?"

"Then," replied the baron, "I command, that, henceforth, thou shalt never receive the knight within the castle."

"Thou dost command!" returned the lady Alwena, smiling.

"Yes, lady; I command."

"And who," returned the lady Alwena, in a haughty tone of defiance, "who will obey the commands of a *murderer?*"

"Ha!" cried the baron, stifling his emotion. He would have answered something; but he knew not what to say: he did not apprehend that lady Alwena could be in possession of proofs; but he was mortified to hear from her lips, for whom, too, he had sacrificed the lady Bertha, the sentence of crimination.

The lady Alwena, with a stern and scornful look, quitted the apartment; and the baron retired to his room, to contemplate the unpleasant occurrences which had passed.

"And is it," cried the baron (as he laid himself on the couch) "is it for these miseries, that I have performed such acts of guilt and enormity! are these the promised enjoyments! these the pleasures, set at so high a value by the witch! deceitful Hag! but I will reproach her severely, for the agonies I have suffered."

CHAPTER X

The Baron's Expostulation with the Hag.

A MONTH elapsed, at the palace of Alwena, before the baron made up his mind to visit the witch of Ravensworth: he hoped, that the conduct of lady Alwena would be altered, and that she would not choose to expose herself and him, to the world; they lived, however, in a state of daily warfare: both equally haughty and imperious, they became the most dreadful scourges to each other; the keenest reproaches, the suggestions of growing hatred, were uttered, reciprocally, from their lips, and contempt and scorn were the feelings they entertained one for the other. It is true, that, at times, as is the case with the wicked, pleasure intervened, and, for a few hours, they agreed tolerably well together; but it was never unmixed with alloy. The baron had now become perfectly well acquainted with the former amours of lady Alwena; he knew, that she was more depraved in her appetites, than the most common strumpet; it was impossible, therefore, for him ever to expect the least happiness with such a woman. In spite of all his wealth, the baron de La Braunch was wretched, and forlorn.

Tired and disgusted with the lady Alwena, the baron sought for repose at the castle of La Braunch, and by his absence from the very woman in whose charms he had hoped to have revelled, and in whose conversation, and esteem, he had hoped a continual source of enjoyment.

One fine evening, wretched in his mind, and disappointed of his hopes, the baron wandered abroad, to take the fresh air, and to contemplate on the events that had lately passed. The night was beautiful; the horizon, coloured with the splendor of the setting sun, invited him to wander further than he intended.

The baron, in his walk, came, unexpectedly, close upon the dwelling of the Hag, and, feeling a lively sense of resentment, for the plagues she had permitted him to suffer, entered her hut.

The witch, although it was summer, was seated on her three-legged stool, at the fire.

The baron viewed her sternly—"Hag," cried he, "'tis now some years since my first visit to this place. I sought, from your power, the power of the devils whom you serve, and the power of witchcraft, the riches and pleasures of the world. Riches, 'tis true, I have obtained; but what are riches, without happiness! I am still miserable, Hag!"

"Miserable!" returned the witch.

"Miserable!"

"The baron de La Braunch miserable! what, with riches, and honours, and the possession of the most beautiful of women too!"

"Yes."

"The lady Alwena."

"Ha!"

"Come, come, thou art ungr
ateful."

"Thou hast deceived me, Hag!"

"Do not be so angry, baron; gently, gently."

"I say, witch, I fear that thou hast deceived me."

"How, pray?"

"Didst thou not promise me enjoyment of my riches?"

"I did;—and hast thou not enjoyment?"

"Of what kind?"

"Sensual enjoyment."

"Ha!"

"All that the wicked can expect."

"The wicked!"

"Ay, baron; be not offended; we know each other: purer pleasures thou didst not think worth the seeking; thou didst wish for the delights of pride, of passion, of ambition, of wealth, of luxury; thou hast them."

"Something still is wanting."

"Thou didst bargain for no more."

"Deceitful Hag!"

"What, wouldst thou have peace and joy?"

"Ay, Hag."

"They are not in the gift of Hell."

"Ah!"

"The fiend, thy master, has them not, himself."

"What, then, have I sacrificed for torments?"

"Ungrateful man! but 'tis ever so. Canst thou not to thy palace? hast thou not seats of velvet, and of down, rich repasts, exquisite wines, music, minstrels, the possession of beauty, and the full power of gratifying all thy lusts? away, and be satisfied."

"Satisfied! and is this all the comfort that thou canst give?"

"Be reasonable, most noble baron. Dost thou desire to murder? wouldst thou kill another infant? wouldst thou act more mischief? perpetrate more horrid deeds? I am thy servant still: but do not ask me, baron, for the rewards of virtue; they are not within my reach."

"I have had enough of horrors."

"What, then, is thy wish with the Hag? is she to soothe thee? to offer comfort to thee? to sing thee hymns and requiems? fie, fie! thou hast chosen to trample down the innocent; to disfigure the face of nature; to strike at virtue; thou hast succeeded wonderfully; and now wouldst thou whimper, like a child, because thou art become fretful, and tired of thy sport? away, away; go home; the lady Alwena waits; she will nurse thee in her bosom."

"Devil, say no more!"

"Nay; be not angry."

"Thou hast buoyed me up in blood, and now thou wouldst leave me to sink in the disgustful stream, without help, or pity."

"Pity! that is an attribute of Heaven; we, baron, do not know it; we enjoy, not pity, the miseries of our fellow creatures."

The baron shrank at the reproach, he said no more; he left the hut.

Oppressed, and sick at heart, the baron pursued the first path he came to, regardless whither he went: he began, now, to abhor the crimes that had produced only torment; he began to hate himself; he began to hate the fair promise of vice, that he had found to be a lie.

CHAPTER XI

Of Gerrard, the Wood-Cutter, and his Wife, Deborah.

IN the south part of the forest, about nine miles from the castle of La Braunch, lived a poor honest wood-cutter, named Gerrard.

Gerrard was not more than thirty years of age, lusty and strong, but of a handsome figure; he was rough, and sturdy, as an oak; but bent as tenderly, to the tale of distress, as the gourd to the wind: he was apt, 'tis true, to be a little ill-tempered, at times, and somewhat sour, besides being a little rude and unfashioned in his manners; but, somehow or other, so finely delineated were the characters of nature and truth in his mind, that he was always kind and courteous, whenever humanity claimed his protection.

Gerrard had a wife, named Deborah.

Deborah was, naturally, a good woman, and very industrious and careful; but apt to fret and scold, whenever Gerrard was out of work, for they had nothing but hard labour to support them, and it was not unfrequently that they were in want even of a meal.

Deborah had no children; but it had happened, unluckily for her and her husband, that they had to support a boy, who was not their own, but who was now of an age to begin to work.

Gerrard was not an ignorant man, although a poor one, for it had happened, that an old friar had taken the pains to teach him to read; but, unfortunately, his wife, Deborah, was the daughter of a once wealthy yeoman, but who had been ruined by a murrain among his cattle; Deborah, therefore, who recollected the plentiful and hospitable board her father kept, was a little discontented at her condition in life: she was not only often repining at her lot, but longing for riches, which, indeed, appeared to her the greatest blessing in life.

It was towards the cottage of these poor people, that the baron, finding himself likely to be overtaken by a sudden tempest, bent his steps. The most beautiful and azure sky, studded with the appearance of many brilliant stars, had become overcast. The light from the cottage of Gerrard, the woodcutter, was the first notice that the baron received, of a shelter near at hand, in case of a storm.

As the baron approached the door of the cottage, he heard voices; it seemed to him, as if it were people scolding at each other.

The subject of their quarrel was riches, poverty.

"My dear," said one of them, "what a passion you are in!"

"I may well be in a passion," answered the other; "this is the last meal we shall have for these three days."

"That's more than you know."

"I am almost famished; I am."

"Look at the poor cat, and be thankful.—Well, there's your supper."

"Supper! do you call it? why, there isn't enough to bait a mouse-trap; I sha'n't touch a morsel."

"Well, now, there's the difference: whilst pride is choking itself with ill-temper, humility sits down, and falls to, with a thankful heart."

"You'd see me starve; you would: you'll make me mad; you will."

"No, my dear; truly you are brought too low for that."

"You brute, you! but it serves me right: I might have married a rich yeoman, that I might, and have lived on the fat of the land."

"Shu!"

"To throw myself on a chopper of wood!"

"A chopper of wood! what to you mean by that?"

"A lazy, idle fellow."

"Truly, I will show my activity forthwith."

The baron knocked at the door; the storm had begun.

"There's some one knocks."

"I am glad of it; then I shall have a witness to your ill-usage."

One of them opened the door.

The baron entered. He addressed himself to a poor labouring man, and to a woman:—"Good people," said he, "will you afford a stranger a few minutes shelter from the storm?"

"Willingly, sir," cried Gerrard, who was a good deal amazed, to see a guest so attired, at his humble cottage.

"Very willingly, sir," cried Deborah; "wo'n't you be pleased to sit down, sir?"

A little boy, who had just awaked from sleep, in a corner of the hut, and who was apprenticed to Gerrard, brought a chair.

"Well, Gerrard," cried the baron, "how is the world wont to use thee; roughly, or passing smooth?"

"Roughly enough, sir, Heaven knows!" cried Deborah.

"Who told you to speak?—My wife, sir, is always grumbling; she must needs be longing for riches; and though I don't remember, by the goodness of Providence, that we have ever wanted a meal, yet she can't be content."

"Ah! 'tis fine talking," replied Deborah; "but nobody knows, but the poor, what poor people suffer."

"Come, come, be better tempered with each other," cried the baron; "and do you think, good woman, that riches make their owners happy?"

"I am sure I don't know, sir," answered Deborah, "why they should not; for rich folks can take their pleasure, and can eat and drink whatever they have a fancy for; and then they can feed ever so many poor people, and make such a power of folks happy."

"Aye, aye, wife; so they might," replied Gerrard, "and yet not be happy, themselves, after all."

"Well, now, I can't see that, for the soul of me," returned Deborah.

"Why," answered Gerrard, "suppose they did not come honestly by their riches?"

The baron shrank at this unmeant reproach.

"Aye, that I don't understand," said Deborah; "I would not keep any thing a moment that I hadn't come by honestly, as soon as I found who was the right owner; but, to be sure, I should like dearly to be rich, and to have a castle, and forests, and deer, of my own, and plenty of servants."

"And are you sure," cried the baron, "that, if you were rich, you would be happy?"

"Happy! aye; that I should, sir; and I would never scold my poor Gerrard again; for he is as good a creature as ever was born, though I was scolding him just now; and, to speak the truth, I don't believe that he could have got any work yesterday, though I did throw it in his teeth, that he did not; but, sir, when one is poor, and when one has no meat in the pot, it puts one out of temper sadly."

Gerrard wiped his eyes, at this kind offer of atonement, and the baron went into a deep reverie.

The storm was over: the baron arose; he pulled out a heavy purse from his pocket; he gave it to Deborah; he wished them both a good night.

Gerrard offered to see the baron through the forest; which he declined to accept.

The instant the baron had left the cottage, Deborah ran to the light, to examine the purse; it was full of gold. "Blessed saint," cried Deborah, "what is this? all gold! Gerrard, look here; see what Providence has done for us!"

"Aye; I told you so," said Gerrard, "and you are always grumbling."

"Nay, now; don't be cross, Gerrard, with so much good luck; look at it again, Gerrard; it is all gold, every bit of it! I'll have a new dress, and poor Henry shall have a new coat."

"And what am I to have?" cried Gerrard.

"You shall see us all clean, and happy."

"Thank'e; well, that will do for me."

"And we will have a good piece of meat in the pot to-morrow."

"And I'm sure you wo'n't sleep to-night."

"That I sha'n't. Well, who knows what luck's to follow?"

"Peace, Deborah! now mayn't this be a temptation?"

"May it, Gerrard?"

"Who knows?"

"If I thought so, I would not touch it."

"Come, come," cried Gerrard; "while it don't make us covetous after more, and lead us to do wrong, we have nothing to fear, Deborah; it will then be a blessing, in spite of the devil; for my part, I shall work the same as ever, only don't grumble, Deborah."

"You shall never hear a cross word from me, Gerrard."

Thus did the cottagers end their discourse, and retire to rest, pleased, and happy with each other.

Very different was the situation of the baron de La Braunch: he returned to the palace of Alwena, just in time to witness a stranger, on horseback, covered with a cloak, and accompanied by two attendants, leave that mansion of pleasure; he had no doubt, but that it was the knight, Alaric; but, as they rode past at full speed, he could not ascertain who they were.

The baron supped with lady Alwena, and then retired, on the score of ill-health, to his own apartment; he retired to suffer the bitterness of remorse: he had now seen himself at the pinnacle of his ambition; he was one of the richest knights in the kingdom; enjoyed a good fame, and the favour of his prince; but he was a wretch, for he had bartered, for those acquisitions, the honesty and dignity of a man: he might have been happy, by the consent of the world, of riches, and of fame; but, the consent of his own heart, to the enjoyment of them, was wanting; he began to find himself so restless and disturbed in the possession of wealth, that he would gladly have parted with it all again, to have been innocent: he had sacrificed the life of lady Bertha, for the possession of a cruel and wanton woman, who tortured and defied him, who reigned sole mistress over his inclinations, and who made of a tyrant, a slave and vassal; the baron had now no home, no resting-place; to wander the face of the earth, like the murderer, Cain, would, to him, have been a solace.

CHAPTER XII

The Baron sends for Father Velaschi.

THE misery of the baron de La Braunch had now become so complete, and his conscience so disturbed, that not any thing could be more pitiable than his situation; day followed day, and hour succeeded hour, without his gaining the smallest portion of rest or repose.

The arrogance of lady Alwena grew, at this time, more and more insupportable; and her intrigues had become so barefaced and public, that the baron was continually disgraced by her enormities.

The baron's holy confessor was the monk Velaschi, apparently the most devout, though suspected, at the same time, of being the greatest hypocrite of his order.

The monk Velaschi was, however, sent for by the baron, and was too great an adept in the knowledge of human nature, not to discover, presently, the state of the baron's mind. He would have brought him to the sacrament of penitence, or, as it is commonly called, confession; but the baron constantly avoided the fulfilment of the monk Velaschi's purpose; every endeavour was in vain.

Although the baron had, himself, sent for the friar, it was not with a desire to attend the confessional; his crimes were of so horrid, and so black a die, that they would not allow him to be explicit; nevertheless, he wished in some way to ease his mind, and to compound with his religion, if possible: he desired, therefore, to sound the monk, on the subject of repentance.

The good father had received the summons, to attend a penitent, with becoming joy; he hastened to the castle of La Braunch, whither the baron had retired, on pretence of having to arrange some concerns of business.

The monk found his penitent a prey to all the horrors of remorse, and nearly in a state of horrid desperation.

The holy confessor administered the comfortable promises of religion: he recited to him the prayer of *Angelus*, both at noon, and in the evening, to the tolling of the convent clock; he repeated, too, many times, the *Pater*, and the *Ave;* he sung the anthem *Regina Cœli*, the psalm *De Profundis*, and the *Requiem æternam*.

The baron, however, took no delight in these seraphic strains; he was sensible that he was an hypocrite to himself, and that he was insincere to his confessor: he would willingly have explained the true state of his mind; but his pride was alarmed; he could not bear the thought of avowing such enormous guilt; and thus he continued to bear the burthen of his sin.

Father Velaschi read all the horror of the baron's mind, in his agitated and distracted looks, in his quick rolling eye, and in the sudden incoherent starts he gave, at certain questions put to him, in their proper order, by the monk.

Father Velaschi waited patiently, courted mildly, and reproved forcibly, to engage the baron to unfold the causes of his affliction, but in vain.

CHAPTER XIII

The Western Turret.

IN the western turret of the castle of La Braunch, was an apartment which had not been entered but once, within the recollection of the oldest domestics of the baron.

Various traditions had been handed down, of murders which had been perpetrated in this place, which was at the further end of the gallery.

It had an iron door, fastened with a massy bar.

To this place the baron was now sometimes seen to retire for hours, when every domestic was forbid to approach that part of the gallery; an injunction which might have been easily spared, as it would have been with great reluctance, if they could have been prevailed upon at all to visit the western turret.

It could not be conjectured, why the baron had chosen this apartment for his meditations; but thither, however, he not only retired, but remained for hours together.

There was not any thing that could have a more gloomy appearance, than the castle of La Braunch; scarcely a female remained within its walls. Ranetrude would have left, soon after her mistress had been missed, and have sought a situation, most likely, where such dismal events might not be expected; she had already given warning. No company now visited the place; and Doric, and Jonas, had scarcely any other employment, than to take care of themselves.

The palace of Alwena was, all this time, the gay resort of the young accomplished knights of the court of Edward, particularly Alaric, who was received by its abandoned mistress with the most distinguished favour, and in open defiance of the orders of the baron de La Braunch.

It might have been expected, that the baron would have challenged this young lord to single combat, after the flagrant proofs he had had of his intrigue with the lady Alwena; but the truth was, that he had become almost indifferent, as to the conduct of that infamous woman, nor did he care much, to wage war with one who knew, but too well, the secrets of his guilt; he contrived, therefore, to treat her with a show of courtesy, in which abominable species of dissimulation she did not allow herself to be outdone.

CHAPTER XIV

The Baron's Dinner with the Lady Alwena, and the Consequences.

THINGS were in this situation with the baron de La Braunch, and the lady Alwena, when, one day, the baron made a formal visit to that lady, with an intention to dine with her at the palace, more to divert his mind from the dreadful recollections with which it was frequently occupied, than from any respect for the gay mistress of that *gay* mansion.

The baron went rather earlier than usual, and found that his lady was dressing in her room; he sent, however, a message, by one of her women, to say that he would do himself the honour to dine with her; which was rather unacceptable tidings to her, as the young Alaric had been already invited, and it was necessary that he should receive a proper notice of the disappointment. Indeed the lady Alwena, who had obtained all that her ambition desired, from the proud alliance she had made with the rich baron de La Braunch, began, notwithstanding, to find him, in the way in which they lived, a severe incumbrance; nor could she, at times, in the wickedness of her heart, help wishing him dead, that she might enjoy, unmolested, the vast wealth of which he was possessed.

During the time of lady Alwena's dressing for dinner, the baron wandered across the forest, until he came to the cottage of Gerrard and Deborah; he entered, and found them both at dinner, with the fine healthy boy, the apprentice of Gerrard, who had returned with his master, from cutting wood in the forest.

The repast of these poor people was frugal; but they seemed to enjoy their humble meal exceedingly, as he had heard them laughing heartily as he approached the door.

"Well," cried the baron to Deborah, "dost thou still continue to long for riches?"

"O yes, sir!" replied the poor woman, "as much as ever; I should like to be rich, of all things; every body should be the better for it, and this poor orphan too."

"I tell my wife," interrupted Gerrard, "that riches would only be a burthen to us; but she wo'n't believe me."

"No; that I wo'n't, Gerrard," answered Deborah; "because it would be our own faults, if we could not enjoy them."

The baron could not help feeling the severity of these unintentional reproaches; but he was in a disposition to desire to suffer, and the misery he endured, was to him a luxury; he knew that he ought not to be blest with peace; and the mortifying dismissal he had received from the Hag, had operated to make him hate and detest himself, and all the world.

The baron, astonished at the avidity of the cottager's wife after wealth, and pleased to find the curse of ambition in one so poor, opened his purse to her, and put the contents of it in her hand, which were received with an ecstasy of joy.

The baron bent his steps towards the palace of Alwena, ruminating, all the way he went, on crimes that were past atonement, and on misery likely to endure through life. "Whither," cried he, "am I going? to a gilded palace, wherein resides a corrupt and hateful harlot, whose beauty and wantonness may invite me to dalliance, but whose embraces are death! Alas! it was my sensual and depraved appetites, that were the first cause of my forsaking the principles of virtue and honour, and the cause of my first crime; it was ambition, and the inordinate desire of wealth, that made me sacrifice a pure and spotless breast, that would have loved me for ever. Well, well! pleasure awaits me, and I will enjoy the hour: lady Alwena is beautiful; and to revel in her charms, is a banquet for a king!"

An elegant repast was prepared, against the return of the baron, and the most delicious wines were poured into the rich golden vases which ornamented the table.

The lady Alwena was adorned in the most superb attire, and her charms were set forth to the greatest advantage; which display was in truth, however, intended for Alaric.

Never was a lady more engaging and attentive, than was the lady Alwena to her lord. The baron forgot, for a while, the hateful retrospect of her misconduct; he thought only of the lovely form seated next him. She drank his health, with the most fascinating smile; which he returned, with all the courtesy of a true-bred knight.

The baron had not taken his wine many minutes, before he found his head begin to swim; a new and dreadful sensation made him shudder, from head to foot;—he perceived that he was poisoned.

"Lady Alwena," cried the baron, dissembling with his usual address, "you had better taste of this Burgundy; the flavour of it is excellent."

The lady Alwena declined, with consummate art.

He pressed her again. She still refused.

The baron looked her full in the face, and insisted on her compliance. She persisted in her refusal.

At length the baron, with a countenance marked with rage, presented the cup to her.

The haughty Alwena arose from her seat, and, with an indignant glance, and stately air, was about to quit the chamber.

"Hold," cried the baron, "thou fiend of Hell!" drawing his sword from the scabbard.

The lady Alwena endeavoured to pass.

He plunged the weapon in her bosom.

She fell back; the blood streamed from her milk-white breasts, and their beauty was overspread with the torrent.

"Wretch!" cried the lady Alwena, as she sank on the earth, "it is one comfort to me, that thou must die also."

The baron leaned his head on his hand. The lady Alwena lay prostrate, at his feet.

"Now," cried the baron, "it is over; and the life ends, for the fancied enjoyments of which, I have forfeited every thing that leads to happiness."

The baron looked down on Alwena. She was dead. Her face was distorted with the rage of her dying hour; her beauty was gone already.

Hathbrand entered; he had come to wait on his lord: he viewed the scene of horror, and would have retired from a spectacle so dreadful, but his legs would not obey the impulse; he was fixed to the spot.

The baron desired to be removed to the castle of La Braunch. He had no sooner reached it, than the signs of death came on.

The baron ordered Hathbrand to bring a parchment scroll from out of his library. The attendant obeyed; the scroll was brought in.

"This scroll," said the baron, fixing his eyes stedfastly upon it, "is my will; I have only to seal it."

"Hathbrand," continued the baron, "thou wilt find, in the forest, a solitary cottage, inhabited by a wood-cutter and his wife.—The name of the wood-cutter is Gerrard. These people are poor; they wish to be rich, and they shall be rich; they shall be the heirs of the baron de La Braunch. Who knows? perhaps, to them, riches may be a blessing: to me, power and riches have been misery and horror."

The baron signed his name at the foot of the parchment scroll, and affixed his seal. It was done in the presence of father Velaschi, and of Hathbrand.

The baron wished to receive the sacrament of extreme unction. All, but the father Velaschi, retired.

It was, however, too late to administer to the penitent: the mind, as well as the body, was dreadfully convulsed.

At length, the sleep of death came on; the haughty baron de La Braunch sunk down towards everlasting misery.

His voice grew faint and tremulous. He spoke:—"The scroll; the western turret; the Hag; the Hag!"

After the holy father Velaschi had given orders, that the body of the baron should be deposited, for three days, in the room of state, he left the castle, giving strict injunctions to Hathbrand, to seek out, without delay, the woodcutter, Gerrard, and his wife, to inform them of their good fortune.

CHAPTER XV

The Wood-cutter, and his Boy.

HATHBRAND crossed the forest, on his errand.

Gerrard was in the woods, at his labour, with his boy, and Deborah directed the esquire to the spot.

On approaching the place, Hathbrand heard voices: one said, in a tone as if scolding—"You little lazy monkey! do you think that I am to keep you for doing nothing? why don't you get another withy, and bind up those faggots?"

"I am at work, as fast as I can," answered the other; "but you are so cross, Gerrard!"

"Cross! I am not cross."

"If you are tired of keeping me, I'll seek for support elsewhere; I'll leave you to-morrow."

"Leave me! that you sha'n't. I found you at my door, one bitter cold night, wrapped up in flannel, a poor helpless brat! It was humanity made me take you in; and though I am apt to be somewhat sour at times, I have a little of the same humanity left, that will never suffer me to turn you out."

"You have been very kind to me; but I am not ungrateful; indeed, I am not; I am always ready to work, when you bid me."

"Truly, so thou art; but I am wont, sometimes, to be illtempered, when things run cross in the grain, or a knot comes in my way. Here, you little rogue! give me your hand, and we will have a drop of beer together."

The woodman and his boy sat down, on the trunk of a tree they had just felled, and were seeking their refreshment from out of a wallet, when the stranger came into the close.

Hathbrand saluted them; and they returned the greeting in the best manner they were able.

Hathbrand took particular notice of the boy: he was handsome, and well-made; he was, however, ragged as a colt.

Hathbrand spoke:—"Come, Gerrard," said he, "thou must leave off work, and return home."

"Truly not yet," answered the honest wood-cutter; "I have not yet quite done work."

"No matter; thou must go with me to the cottage; I have good news to tell thee."

"Good news! but I must know what it is, before I budge; is it worth half a day's work?"

"Truly it is; and a twelvemonth's work too."

"Nay, if that be the case, I'm your man; so here's pack up." The boy followed.

On their arrival at the cottage, they found Deborah at home, who prepared a place for the stranger.

Hathbrand prefaced what he had to say, with some remarks on the extraordinary changes and vicissitudes of human life; and then inquired of them, if they recollected the circumstance of a stranger, of more than ordinary appearance, having visited them some time before.

Gerrard and Deborah, by turns, recounted the adventures of that evening, and related the munificence the stranger displayed.

"Now then," cried Hathbrand, "I know that you are truly the people whom I seek. Prepare to go with me to the castle of La Braunch, thou, and thy wife, and all thy family."

"Indeed, sir, you will excuse me there," cried Gerrard; "I shall not stir out any more to day."

"Foolish man!" returned Hathbrand; "know, then, that the stranger, who visited thee, was the baron de La Braunch; he is dead; and, more, thou art heir to all his rich demesnes."

"I don't rightly understand you, sir," cried the wood-cutter.

"The castle, the lands, all the real and personal estate of the late baron de La Braunch, are thine."

"My dear, you don't seem to understand the gentleman," cried Deborah.

"Not I, in good faith."

"Why, bless me! don't you hear that you have got to be a rich man? and that the baron, who came here, one tempestuous night, has left you all that he was worth in the world?"

"Well! and what will become of me? what am I to do with so much riches?"

"Do with it, husband! give it to me, if you don't know what to do with it; I warrant I'll find a way to lay it out."

"I don't want to be put out of my way," replied Gerrard.

Poor Deborah, in the simplicity of her heart, stopped her husband's mouth. "Lord! Gerrard, don't affront the gentleman; I am sure that I should like to be a lady very much; and to be sure, I did think that there was something very odd in the stranger's behaviour to us, and that he meant to do something for us; though to be sure,

I did not think that he would die, and leave us all his wealth; but this gentleman would not say so, if it were not true; so, Gerrard, if you needs must be a rich man after all, why, you know that you must not mind a little trouble."

"Well!" replied Gerrard, "if it must be so, there's no help for it."

Hathbrand had provided a cloak, with a hat and sword, with which he accoutred the wood-cutter; and a decent robe, which he threw over the shoulders of Deborah.

The boy was to stay at home, to take care of the cottage; but the poor lad seemed very much disconcerted at first, at being left: he was, however, a good-hearted youth; and, when he recollected that it was owing to his master's good fortune, he forgot every thing else.

CHAPTER XVI

Gerrard and Deborah's Arrival at the Castle.

IT was late in the evening, when Gerrard, and his wife, Deborah, arrived at the castle of La Braunch.

The strangers were conducted to an elegant room, prepared for their reception by the careful Hathbrand, who, in hopes of being retained in office, was as courteous and polite to them, as he had been to his deceased lord.

Hathbrand immediately caused one of the wardrobes of the deceased baron to be opened, from whence he selected some of the plainest attire, such as he thought would, at first, best become their sudden and unexpected change of circumstances.

Deborah, however, was extremely desirous of being fine; she loved to be drest, and could not be prevailed on, to put on any thing but the most gaudy apparel in the wardrobe. She was extremely pleased with the attentions of her waiting-woman, Ranetrude, who had offered her services, and, except the novelty of having nothing to do for herself, she was under less restraint than could have been expected.

The inhabitants of the castle were all alive with the news of the arrival of their new lord and lady; and were impatient to pay their respects; in this, however, they were disappointed, for that night. Doric, the old steward, and Jonas, the butler, received orders to attend, with the rest of the servants, the next morning, in the hall, to hear their late master the baron's will read, and to receive their new lord and lady.

The story had already got wind, that the baron de La Braunch had left his immense possessions to a poor wood-cutter, and many and numerous were the remarks and low witticisms on the occasion, from old Doric, Jonas the butler, and the other servants.

The next day, the numerous tenantry of the baron, who had also been summoned to attend, met at the hall, and, with the domestics, waited in eager expectation, to see their new master, Gerrard, and their lady, Deborah.

At length the folding doors, leading from the staircase, were thrown open, and Gerrard and Deborah, attended by Hathbrand and Ranetrude, entered the hall. Gerrard bowed his head without awkwardness, and stept forward without dismay. Deborah assumed an air of vast consequence; yet she did not look unkind on any: she was filled with notions of her situation; but was naturally social and kind; and, if she had not considered that it would be improper, she would gladly have been familiar.

Hathbrand held the parchment scroll in his hand; he spoke:—"My good friends, peace be with you all! I here produce the will of your late master, the baron de La Braunch. Attend.—'Know all men, that I, the baron de La Braunch, lord of all the demesnes in and about Ravensworth, do hereby give and bequeath to Gerrard Le Blanc, of the forest, wood-cutter, all the real and personal estate of which I now stand possessed, upon condition that he shall, on the seventh day after my decease, take possession of the castle, and that, when the clock shall have struck twelve, at midnight of that day, he shall go, alone, into the chamber of the western turret, where he will find the title-deeds to such estates.'"

The instant that the western turret was named, a rumour was immediately heard among the domestics.

Gerrard took little notice of the sensation which had been expressed among the servants; he was firm, and unconscious of any thing to fear. Deborah, however, felt a little uneasiness; her curiosity, and her fears for Gerrard, were both excited.

Gerrard addressed the tenantry:—"Friends and neighbours, Providence has so ordered it, that a poor wood-cutter should become your lord. There be many who would find it difficult to do their duty in a station so much above them: I shall not; I shall be just and honest, and it must go hard indeed, if things turn out amiss. You shall all be rich in the best comforts of life, and the poor man shall never want bread. I am now, as it were, the great oak of the forest, and the unfortunate shall always find a shelter beneath the wide-spreading branches of English hospitality. I shall give judgment among you fairly. I have not much learning, 'tis true, yet, I know that there is but the right and the wrong, and that it is not so easy to mistake one for the other, as many people would try to make us believe. Keep in your own stations; don't dispute the rights of your great neighbours, and they shall not trample on yours. Gerrard, your new master, will as far as in him lies, protect the weak, strike at the root of corruption, and fell oppression to the ground."

Three successive shouts succeeded this noble harangue of Gerrard, the honest wood-cutter.

After the ceremony of taking possession was over, Gerrard, whose heart was too good to let him enjoy the good things prepared at his sumptuous board, while disturbed with the reflection, that one of his family, whom he loved too, was left in a state of anxiety and uneasiness—it was his poor boy, Henry; and he now dispatched a domestic to the cottage, with orders to bring him to the castle, that he might also partake of the promised festivity. The domestic returned, in about three hour, but it was without the boy: the boy had left the cottage; the cottage was empty.

Gerrard had never felt any thing that had given him so much uneasiness before.

"My poor boy gone!" cried Gerrard; "my poor foundling! what shall I do? I'll go and seek him, myself; I'll search through the forest; poor fellow! but I'll go and see for him, myself. He was the kindest child! but hold; perhaps he is gone to father Velaschi; the good old monk was always fond of him; I dare say he is there; I'll go and see.

Hathbrand represented to the honest wood-cutter, the impropriety of his leaving the castle at such a time; besides, that the hour approached for him to pay his visit to the chamber in the western turret, in conformity with the injunctions of the will of the baron de La Braunch.

Deborah also endeavoured to persuade her husband that the boy was safe. The good father Velaschi was expected; the boy would come with him. He had taught him to read, and was never so happy, as when he was giving him instruction.

Gerrard was ill satisfied with these conjectures; he was assured that some accident had happened to him; the poor boy had thought that they had deserted him; he had left the cottage a wanderer; he would never return.

Gerrard gave orders, that two of the domestics should go different ways, in search of the youth. He was obeyed with alacrity.

CHAPTER XVII

The Supper.—Gerrard's Visit to the Western Turret.

DORIC, the honest old steward, and his friend Jonas, the butler, had taken most especial care, to be as superb and expensive, in the preparations for his new master's supper, as if the baron had been alive. Their sentiments, too, had been all at once changed about their new master: he was a fine, brave, noble fellow; and they were sure, that he would take care, that they should be, all of them, happy and comfortable; and it was but proper, that they should show him all the respect and homage in their power.

The waiting-lady, Mrs. Ranetrude, and the women servants, were not less delighted with their new mistress. The fact was, that, though she was somewhat vulgar, she was naturally of a kind disposition; and, though she was, as might have been expected, extremely proud of her new situation, and fine dress, yet she was not arrogant, and her generosity blunted the shafts of ridicule. They found that they had a true friend in their mistress, and were wise and grateful enough, to think that she was every thing to them.

The supper was ready; the table was spread with such delicacies as had never before been seen by the honest Gerrard, or his wife, Deborah.

They sat down to the entertainment. Hathbrand was with them. Doric and Jonas waited.

A minstrel had also been invited, to play them the most favourite ballads.

Gerrard appeared thoughtful and low-spirited. Hathbrand, to do him justice, used every means in his power, to keep up the spirits of his new master.

"Truly," cried Gerrard, "I was never much given to superstition; but, somehow or other, whenever the western turret is mentioned, my blood chills at once."

"Doubtless," returned Hathbrand, "some mystery hangs about the circumstances of that place, which the extraordinary injunction in the baron's will confirms; such, however, are the terms on which the tenure of your large demesnes depends."

"Well, then, be it so," returned Gerrard.

Poor Deborah was so much delighted with the sumptuous repast, which had been prepared for her, that she had not heard a syllable of what had passed between her husband and Hathbrand; her eyes were the organs most engaged, and her taste was the sense next gratified; no time was allowed for attention to the conversation.

A silent moment ensued: the hour began to approach fast, for Gerrard to visit the western turret.

The domestics were engaged in one corner of the hall, talking the matter over.

"I'd be shot if I'd go," cried Doric, as he tossed off a cup of Burgundy.

"He must be drunk, if he attempts it," returned Jonas, scarcely able to stand.

Gerrard started from a reverie:—"Well, I am poor, and the temptation's strong. I have often worked alone in the woods; but then, viewing the cheerful sun, and the flowers, and the trees, and the green shrubs, my heart was always glad, and rejoiced. I don't know how it is, that I am so much depressed about going to a room alone. I never injured any body: what have I to fear? Good Providence, shield me from harm!"

"Lord! Gerrard," interrupted Deborah, "do not go, if you think that any harm will happen to you; let us go back again to our humble cottage: what would be the use of all the riches in the world, if we were not happy? and what would be all the wealth of this castle, if I were to lose my Gerrard?"

"Never fear, Deborah; never fear, my girl," replied Gerrard.

The hour drew nigh: it wanted but half an hour.

Hathbrand filled a goblet of wine; he drank to Gerrard.

Gerrard returned a health to Hathbrand, and to all.

It wanted a quarter only.

Gerrard looked at the clock; a silence ensued.

It wanted but ten minutes of the time; no one spoke.

The clock struck twelve.

Gerrard started from his seat:—"Give me the light," cried he; "I'll go instantly:" he took the taper in his hand.

"Deborah," cried he, "farewell! in a few minutes, I shall return."

"God bless you, Gerrard!"

"Aye; God bless you, indeed!" repeated Doric.

"We shall never see him any more," cried Jonas.

Deborah did not hear the words; her heart was full: she returned to the supper-table.

A pause succeeded the departure of Gerrard; all was still and silent.

CHAPTER XVIII

The Western Turret.

GERRARD explored his way; for the single taper in his hand gave but a feeble light, the whole length of the gallery, and of the winding stair-case of the castle.

A high wind had sprung up, followed by a tempest; the rain beat against the windows; the thunder rolled at a distance, and lightnings began to flash. The figures of the tapestry, in the rooms through which he passed, seemed to move. Gerrard was undaunted.

At length he ascended the steps which led to the western turret, and, following the directions which had been given him, arrived at the iron door. The massy key, which he held in his hand, fitted the lock; it was in vain, however, that he attempted to open it. He made several unsuccessful efforts; at length, by main strength only, he turned the key, and the door fell open.

There was a light in the room; it was one solitary lamp.

In the midst of the chamber was a bier; a figure of a woman was laid on it.

A cradle stood next the bier; the figure of an infant also was placed in the cradle.

Gerrard started back with terror. He took, however, the taper in his hand, and approached nearer to the objects he had beheld. There appeared no life in the bodies.

Gerrard was exploring the room, to find the chest, in which, he supposed, were kept the deeds containing the title of the baron, when he discovered a parchment scroll, suspended from one end of the bier. There was inscribed on it, in large letters—*"The Title of the Baron de La Braunch to the Demesnes of Ravensworth."*

Gerrard snatched the scroll from the bier, and read—*"Know, unhappy wretch who longest after riches! that the title to these demesnes is murder."*

"Murder!" repeated Gerrard. He trembled from head to foot, as he repeated the word murder; he cast his eyes involuntarily on the dead bodies; he staggered against the wall.

The high wind rushed along the floor of the chamber; the taper was nearly extinguished with the gusts from the arras; the light burnt dim; the flame tapered, and the point vibrated with the motion.

Gerrard felt a chill of horror. He cast his eyes again on the body of the female on the bier: the face was pale, and blood appeared on the bosom. He looked at the infant: the face of the child, too, was pale; but there was no blood.

Gerrard retired from the chamber.

CHAPTER XIX

The Return of Gerrard to the Supper-table.—The Scroll.—The last Appearance of the Hag.

DEBORAH was leaning her cheek upon her hand, listening, in the most anxious suspense.

Hathbrand was wrapt up in thought.

"What a stormy night!" exclaimed Doric.

"It blows a whirlwind," answered Jonas.

Deborah broke silence:—"I thought that I heard him coming. Alas! it is not him."

"Be comforted, my dear lady," replied Ranetrude; "my master will return presently."

Deborah fetched a heavy sigh.

Footsteps were heard in the gallery; it was some one descending the stairs.

They were the footsteps of Gerrard.

He entered.

He spoke:—"Deborah!" was all that he could utter.

He fell into a chair, and dropped the scroll.

"Heavens! what ails you, Gerrard?" exclaimed Deborah. "Speak, speak to me, Gerrard."

"Let us to our cottage, Deborah, let us to our cottage, my girl: read, read, read!"

Hathbrand took up the scroll of parchment; he read

"The Confessions of the Baron de La Braunch.
Know, unhappy wretch, who longest after riches! that the title to these estates is murder."

"Murder!" was reverberated through the hall.

Hathbrand continued:—"The infant Edward, the rightful heir to the demesnes of Ravensworth, was murdered by the Hag, at the instance of the baron de La Braunch. The lady Bertha, too, was afterwards made away with, at his instigation, and by means of the same accursed instrument. But the crimes of the baron were of a much earlier date; for, after seducing lady Gertrude, the child of lord Hubert, he destroyed the object of his seduction by means of poison, through the aid of the monk, his confessor."

"Horrible!" cried Gerrard.

"Horrible, indeed!" repeated Deborah.

"It is now just eleven years," cried Hathbrand, "since the child, Edward, was missed from the castle."

"The Hag was always suspected," interrupted Ranetrude.

"The Hag is still alive," cried Gerrard; "let her be brought instantly to justice."

It was the first command that Gerrard had given in the castle, with anger on his brow.

Hathbrand was preparing to obey the order of his new master, when, on a sudden, the folding-doors of the inner hall opened with a dreadful crash.

Three figures, entirely covered with black mantles, appeared at the entrance.

The middle one was the Hag.

She uncovered her face.

The other two remained covered.

A sudden dread overcame all who were present.

The Hag advanced forward.

"Accursed witch!" cried Gerrard, "the wicked instrument of the baron's enormities, answer me."

"I will," replied the witch.

"Thou art accused of the murder of the lady Bertha's child, lord Edward: nay, more—of the murder of lady Bertha."

"One thing at a time," replied the Hag.

"Say, wretch! art thou guilty, or not?"

"As you please."

"Nay, answer me, or the most dreadful torture shall extort a confession from thee."

"Who is my accuser?" replied the Hag.

"Thy master, wretch! the baron himself."

Hathbrand held up the scroll.

"Now then," continued Gerrard, "what hast thou to say?"

"Peace a little," cried the witch: "thou hast made thy speech; it is my turn now to speak. Thou hast no power to harm the Hag; but I will answer thee; I am prepared; here are my witnesses."

The figures in the black mantles came forward: they were still covered.

"Now then to thy questions," continued the Hag; "and first, for the infant. The Hag received the child a present from the baron—a sacrifice."

"A sacrifice!" exclaimed Deborah.

"A sacrifice!" repeated Gerrard.

"A sacrifice," returned the witch. "Was it not mine then, to do with as I pleased? to destroy, or save it?"

"Save it!" cried Gerrard.

"Aye, save it. Suppose the child lives."

"Lives!"

"Aye; lives. Suppose the Hag, the wicked, the accursed Hag, laid it down, covered in flannel, at the door of a poor wood-cutter, in the forest."

"A wood-cutter!"

"Suppose she saw it taken in to shelter."

"Taken in!"

"Aye; but you'll doubt my story; you'll say, that——"

"When did this happen?" interrupted Gerrard.

"Eleven years ago," returned the witch; "one cold night, the twenty-seventh of March."

"Good Heavens!" cried Gerrard; "it was one night in March that I found my poor boy, whom I named Henry, wrapped up in flannel—but this story is well known to some in the forest, and the Hag would fain use it to her purpose."

"I have a witness," returned the Hag.

"Produce him."

The Hag withdrew the mantle from one of the figures. A youth, sumptuously attired, presented himself.

"Now then," cried the Hag, "do you know him? behold the heir to the demesnes of Ravensworth!"

Gerrard answered not a word; he was petrified with astonishment.

Deborah knew the child.

Henry, now lord Edward, spoke to his old master. He was convinced.

"Now then," cried the Hag, "go on. I am accused of the lady Bertha. I have a witness here too; a witness that none can deny."

She drew the mantle from the next figure.

It was the lady Bertha.

"Behold," said the witch, "your mistress! restored to you safe."

Hathbrand knelt down; the servants knelt at her feet: they were transported with joy.

"This, too," cried the Hag, "is my work."

"It is wonderful," replied Gerrard; "it is the hand of Providence!"

"Prepare for more wonders yet," interrupted the witch.

All were silent, and in suspense.

"The baron lives."

"Lives!" repeated Hathbrand.

At this moment father Velaschi entered.

"And here comes my witness, to prove it," continued the Hag.

"It is true," cried the monk, "the baron lives; but is dead to the world: he has taken to a religious life, and hopes, by prayer and penance, to obtain pardon for his intended crimes. The baron was not poisoned; for the mixture given by lady Alwena, had been presented to her by the Hag, on the night of the ball, and was composed of a powder, alarming in its effects, but not fatal. After the holy sacrament had been administered, I relieved the wretched mind of the penitent by—'The child and the lady Bertha are yet alive.'"

"From two horrid murders, then," cried Gerrard, "he is freed. And even yet, of another is he guilty—the lady Gertrude."

"He is not guilty even of that," interrupted the Hag.

"He has confessed it; it is in the scroll."

"He is not guilty."

"Not guilty!"

"The lady Gertrude lives."

At these words, the Hag threw from her the black mantle with which she was covered; a foul and ugly mask also, at the same instant, fell from her face. A female of the most lovely feature, and angelic form, stood upright, attired in white and sumptuous apparel. Nothing more of deformity was seen.

The figure spoke:—"I am lady Gertrude."

A pause of wonder ensued.

"Yes," continued the figure; "the Hag was lady Gertrude. Under the foul and tattered raiment of a witch, lady Gertrude has avenged her wrongs; she has preserved the innocent. In this good work, the ever to be revered father Velaschi has had his share.

"Deceived by specious pretences, and by a false ceremony of the marriage ritual, in Normandy, lady Gertrude suffered all the agony of insulted honour.

"As soon as she discovered, from the baron's lips, that she had been imposed on, she fled to England.

"The baron, too, came to the same shore.

"She was about to appeal to the king for redress.

"The baron laid a plan to poison her.

"It was the monk, Velaschi, who was entrusted with the plot.

"He, the good father Velaschi, revealed the horrible design.

"It was given out, that the poison had done its work.

"It was by his contrivance that it was averted.

"Lady Gertrude left the world alive.

"It was in the deserted castle, that the monk, Velaschi, furnished her a retreat.

"It was visited only at night, by a few of the brotherhood.

"The lights sometimes seen at midnight, gave rise to the belief of its being frequented by devils.

"The castle had a subterraneous passage to the hut, where lady Gertrude always appeared the Hag. But her deformity was only in her mask, her gloves, and mantle. At night she retired to the castle.

"It was the monk Velaschi, who, with the assistance of the brotherhood, contrived all the supernatural appearances, and visions, shown to the baron; the horrid images of wax; the loathsome figure of lady Gertrude, a corpse.

"The fiend, too, was father Velaschi."

Every tongue was silent, during this wonderful discourse, every eye was fixed on lady Gertrude.

She continued:—

"In this retreat she watched the wayward actions of the cruel baron, assisted to prevent his designs, and, by means of aiding the impulse of vice, retarded crime.

"The Hag acquired an ascendancy over the baron, which gave to her all his secrets.

"She knew that he would attempt the murder of the infant, and seconded the design, that she might save its life. She did so; she gave it life, and liberty. Labour bestowed health and strength; and the good monk, Velaschi, watched over the progress of his mind.

"The Hag, too, was the kindest friend of lady Bertha, by appearing her greatest enemy.

"It was the Hag who plunged her in misery, to save and bless her.

"It was the Hag who concealed her in the deserted castle.

"It was the Hag who presented the powder to the wretched lady Alwena.

"Thus has she, by assisting to ravish the infant from its mother, saved that infant's life.

"The Hag watched its rising years, while a wood-cutter's boy.

"Father Velaschi, who ever noticed the children of the poor, gave the child the rudiments of learning.

"It was thus the Hag, as a second means in the hands of Providence, prevented evil, and brought forth good.

"The purpose is effected.

"The wretched lady Alwena only has suffered.

"The wicked baron was not guilty.

"But a still greater work is yet performed:—It was the Hag who turned the heart of the baron de La Braunch, by showing him the contempt and derision of the fiend whom he worshipped, for the miseries he endured, and the mortifying disappointment which ever attends the completion of a crime.

"It was the Hag, too, who, lastly, revenged lady Gertrude's wrongs, and who made that revenge a blessing to her seducer."

Lady Bertha, Edward, Gerrard, Deborah, Hathbrand, Ranetrude, all knelt, and kissed the hand of lady Gertrude.

Father Velaschi laid his hands on them; he blessed them with the benediction of Heaven.

Gerrard gave up instant possession of the castle of La Braunch for the young lord Edward.

The child Edward took hold of Gerrard's hand.—"Thou shalt labour no more in the woods, Gerrard: thou didst always spare me a handful, from thy little means; and ought I not to help thee plentifully from so rich a store!"

Lady Bertha embraced her young lord.

The domestics gave way to festivity; in which they were joined by the good father Velaschi.

The lady Gertrude, after the wonders she had performed, retired to a convent.

The good were not hurt: the bad repented.

FINIS.

NOTES

Page

3   **second crusade:** The mention of the second crusade here is at odds with the reign of Edward mentioned in Chapter II. Edward ruled from 1272 until 1307. The second crusade took place over a century earlier. Nevertheless, Edward did lead a crusade to the Holy Land immediately before he became the monarch, so the 1270s is perhaps the period Brewer had in mind for his novel. The Westmorland setting places the story in the northwest of England, an area that, in Brewer's day, was best known for the Lake District, the popular haunt of Wordsworth, Coleridge, and Southey.

6   **Libellulæ:** dragonfly
    Norman conquest: The Battle of Hastings in 1066 marks the beginning of Norman control in England. The Castle of La Braunch, therefore, is roughly 200 years old.

12   **virginal:** a keyed musical instrument set in a box with no legs. The instrument was popular in England in the 16th and 17th centuries.

14   **EO TRIOMPHE:** most likely a variation of "io triumphe," an exclamation of triumph.

20   **demesnes:** possessions, often used in relation to property or estates.

21   **accouchement:** lying-in; delivery of a child.

22   **font:** receptacle for holy water.

23   **Ethelred:** the appearance of a Saxon name in Norman England is just one more example of the novel's imprecise use of historical setting.
    Corporis mysterium: mystery of the body.

24   **Benedictus Deus:** blessed be God.
    Oremus: the invitation to prayer.
    Lucis Creator Optime: a hymn in praise of the first day of creation, the creation of light.

44   **withy:** a flexible branch, usually willow.

55   **six feet four inches in height:** These are truly Amazonian proportions. The average height of a woman in medieval England was a little over 5' 1" (see Christopher Daniell. Death and Burial in Medieval England 1066-1550. London: Routledge, 1997).

62   **horrid mysteries:** the title of one of the "horrid novels" mentioned by Isabella Thorpe in Jane Austen's *Northanger Abbey*.

        This day se'nnight: one week (seven nights) from this day.

65   **granate:** the word could be a misspelling of "granite," or it could suggest the alter is made of a red (garnet-colored) stone.

73   **tilters:** jousters.

75   **falchions:** swords.

        justs: a variant of "jousts".

76   **fillet:** a headband.

91   **Angelus:** a short devotion in honor of the Incarnation repeated in the morning, noon, and evening; Pater and Ave: the Pater Noster ("Our Father," the beginning of the Lord's Prayer) and Ave Maria (Hail Mary); Regina Cœli: Queen of Heaven, the opening words of the Eastertide anthem of the Blessed Virgin; De Profundis: "out of the depths," the first words of Psalm 129; Requiem œternam: or Requiem aeternam ("eternal rest"), part of the Office of the Dead.

96   **sacrament of extreme unction:** a sacrament to give comfort and spiritual guidance to the seriously ill.

CONTEMPORARY REVIEW OF THE NOVEL

Mr. George Brewer, author of a highly interesting volume, called *Hours of Leisure,* to which we have some time since paid a just tribute of applause, has published a novel called *The Hag!* [*sic*]. It is peculiarly adapted for the amusement of those readers who are fond of extravagancies; and though it is beneath the talents of such a writer as Mr. Brewer, yet it will hold a respectable rank amongst works of fancy.

— *Flowers of Literature* (1808-09): lxxiii.

Printed in the United States
124184LV00001B/85-87/A

9 780976 604884